A Whisker in

the Dark

BOOKS BY LEIGHANN DOBBS

MYSTIC NOTCH (CAT COZY MYSTERY SERIES)

A Twist in the Tail
Ghostly Paws
A Spirited Tail
A Mew to a Kill
Paws and Effect
Probable Paws
A Whisker of a Doubt

BLACKMOORE SISTERS (COZY MYSTERY SERIES)

Dead Wrong
Dead & Buried
Dead Tide
Buried Secrets
Deadly Intentions
A Grave Mistake
Spell Found
Fatal Fortune
Hidden Secrets

LEXY BAKER (COZY MYSTERY SERIES)

Lexy Baker Cozy Mystery Series Boxed Set Vol 1 (Books 1–4)

Or buy the books separately:

Killer Cupcakes
Dying for Danish
Murder, Money and Marzipan
3 Bodies and a Biscotti
Brownies, Bodies and Bad Guys

Bake, Battle and Roll
Wedded Blintz
Scones, Skulls & Scams
Ice Cream Murder
Mummified Meringues
Brutal Brulee (Novella)
No Scone Unturned
Cream Puff Killer
Never Say Pie

KATE DIAMOND MYSTERY ADVENTURES

Hidden Agemda (Book 1)
Ancient Hiss Story (Book 2)
Heist Society (Book 3)

SILVER HOLLOW (PARANORMAL COZY MYSTERY SERIES)

A Spell of Trouble (Book 1)
Spell Disaster (Book 2)
Nothing to Croak About (Book 3)
Cry Wolf (Book 4)
Shear Magic (Book 5)

MOOSEAMUCK ISLAND (COZY MYSTERY SERIES)

A Zen for Murder
A Crabby Killer
A Treacherous Treasure

HAZEL MARTIN (HISTORICAL MYSTERY SERIES)

Murder at Lowry House (Book 1)
Murder by Misunderstanding (Book 2)

LADY KATHERINE REGENCY MYSTERIES

An Invitation to Murder (Book 1)
The Baffling Burglaries of Bath (Book 2)
Murder at the Ice Ball (Book 3)
A Murderous Affair (Book 4)

SAM MASON MYSTERIES (WRITING AS L. A. DOBBS)

Telling Lies (Book 1)
Keeping Secrets (Book 2)
Exposing Truths (Book 3)
Betraying Trust (Book 4)
Killing Dreams (Book 5)

LEIGHANN DOBBS

A Whisker in the Dark

GRAND CENTRAL
PUBLISHING

NEW YORK · BOSTON

Copyright © 2019 by Leighann Dobbs
Cover design: Debbie Clement. Cover Images: Shutterstock.
Cover copyright © 2021 by Hachette Book Group, Inc.

Grand Central Publishing
Hachette Book Group
1290 Avenue of the Americas, New York, NY 10104
grandcentralpublishing.com
twitter.com/grandcentralpub

First published in 2019 by Bookouture, an imprint of StoryFire Ltd.

First Grand Central Publishing edition: January 2021

Grand Central Publishing is a division of Hachette Book Group, Inc. The Grand Central Publishing name and logo is a trademark of Hachette Book Group, Inc.

The publisher is not responsible for websites (or their content) that are not owned by the publisher.

The Hachette Speakers Bureau provides a wide range of authors for speaking events. To find out more, go to www.hachettespeakersbureau.com or call (866) 376-6591.

Library of Congress Cataloging-in-Publication Data has been applied for.

ISBN: 978-1-5387-3621-0 (mass market)

Printed in the United States of America

CW

10 9 8 7 6 5 4 3 2 1

A Whisker in the Dark

Chapter One

I'm fairly certain that having a guest die before break-fast is a once-in-a-lifetime event. Even so, I was feeling a bit nervous as the guests at my newly acquired Oyster Cove Guesthouse dug in. Never mind that the memory of how a previous breakfast had been spoiled in a most alarming manner was still fresh in my mind, the reason I was nervous about *this* breakfast was that I was try-ing out a new pumpkin-bread recipe on my guests and, seeing as my culinary skills were meager at best, I was worried they might not like it.

My worries were not unfounded. Though the guests had filled their plates, the brown loaf sat on the antique mahogany serving table, alone and uncut, shoved to the side like an overweight schoolboy on the playground. It was probably because of the dark edges. Admittedly, I'd left it in the oven a bit too long. Who knew that baking had to be that precise? But it was important I get this right. Millie Sullivan, my mother's best friend and the guesthouse's previous owner, had stressed the fact that having a winning loaf cake to serve at the town's 250-year celebration would be vital to the future of the guesthouse. And, since all my retirement savings were tied up in the purchase of the place, I very much wanted it to have a good future.

I eyed the room with satisfaction. It was the lavish dining room of the grand old mansion that was now a bed-and-breakfast, boasting a twelve-foot ceiling, ornate green-and-gold wallpaper and a gigantic green oriental rug. Ten-foot-tall Palladian windows with a coveted view of the sparkling Atlantic Ocean ringed the far wall. They were open, causing the sheers lining the inside of the gold-and-green silk drapes to flutter from a cooling, salty sea breeze.

On the buffet, eggs steamed in a warming tray, toast glistened with melted butter, bacon practically sizzled on its platter and pancakes dripped with maple syrup. But, more importantly, all the guests were accounted for, so there would be no chance of discovering that one of them had met their maker in a most unsavory manner inside my establishment. It wasn't so much the welfare of the guests themselves I was worried about, more that I didn't want to get a reputation for being a place where people only checked out in a body bag.

It was a positive sign that the two resident cats, Nero and Marlowe, weren't wailing like they'd done a few weeks ago to announce said dead body. In fact, it was relatively quiet, the only sounds the faint cry of gulls drifting in through the window and the far-off sounds of hammering from my carpenter, Ed O'Hara, as he worked to renovate one of the dilapidated sections of the mansion.

I had nothing to worry about other than that no one seemed to want my pumpkin bread. Unless it was the concern that a brawl might break out among the guests. I should have known it could be troublesome to rent all the rooms to one peculiar family—especially one that was in business together. Making cheese sculptures. Yes, you heard me. The Biddefords had a cheese-sculpture business. You'd wonder how that would sustain a whole family, but apparently cheese sculptures were quite popular for parties. I mean, who didn't want a swan carved from a block of Swiss or a rendition of Michelangelo's David chiseled from Muenster on their dining table?

I hadn't known they were peculiar when they checked in. I thought it was kind of cute that the descendants of the shipping magnate who had built the mansion wanted to stay in it for the town's 250-year celebration. Jedediah Biddeford had been an important figure in town back then, and even though ownership of the mansion had passed out of the Biddeford family a couple hundred years ago, I guess they still felt a kinship with it.

How was I supposed to know that every member of the family seemed to have a grudge against the next? From what I could gather— not that I was eavesdropping or anything but sometimes one overhears things by accident—their animosity was a combination of sibling rivalry and jockeying for position in the company. It was all nice-nice on the surface, but I could feel the tensions boiling underneath.

The family had requested that I push the individual tables for four that dotted the antique room together to form one long table. Seemed like a good idea to me since there were no guests other than Biddefords. So there they sat, plates loaded with the sumptuous breakfast for which the guesthouse was known. All homemade, of course, except the pancakes. I confess I made those from a mix.

Doris Biddeford, the matriarch, sat at the head, a look of disapproval on her face as she surveyed her children. She had to be eighty if she was a day. The "children" were in their fifties and I couldn't really say I blamed Doris for scowling. Her kids left a bit to be desired.

Doris's critical gaze zoned in on one of her daughters, Paula. Paula was in her mid-fifties but had the look of someone who'd had more than their share of late nights. Not surprising, though—I could tell Paula liked to imbibe. In fact, as I watched, she retrieved a little nip bottle out of her purse and dumped the entire contents into her coffee.

Seated across from Paula was her brother Earl, who, along with his wife, Arlene, was precisely the opposite of Paula. Fastidiously groomed, they both wore expensive clothes, and Arlene's hair was perfectly coiffed, her fingers glittered with bejeweled rings. Their expressions echoed the mother's disapproval.

"Honestly, Paula, can't you get through one day without the help of Mr. Jack Daniel?" Earl asked.

"Shows how much you know, that wasn't Jack Daniel's, it was Baileys Irish Cream. I would never mix Jack with coffee." Paula hiccupped and practically fell off her chair.

Doris rolled her eyes and shook her head. "Earl's right, you need to straighten up. No wonder the business is going down the crapper."

Earl turned to his mother. "Mom, it is not going down the *crapper*." He glanced back at me as if he was thinking they shouldn't be airing their dirty laundry in front of the innkeeper. It would have been prudent to quietly fade into the hallway so as not to witness the family argument that appeared to be brewing, but I was nosy. Besides, I liked to know who was arguing with whom under my roof, just to keep an eye out for any trouble.

"Might as well be, with all you shady characters running it," added Bob, the other son, who I'd determined was the black sheep of the family. Unlike Earl, who dressed to the nines in designer clothing and Italian leather footwear, Bob was wearing a navy-blue hoodie, jeans and sneakers with the laces undone. He was probably in his late forties and had salt-and-pepper hair that swooped over his forehead in a comb-over. I don't know if he was just a sloppy dresser or trying to look younger, but his clothing choices did nothing for him. It was no surprise, given the way he dressed, that Bob didn't appear to have a significant other.

Carla, the other sister, gave Bob a raised brow. "Like you should talk. You're the one who has a suspicious past."

I could tell Carla was the most normal one of the bunch. But that wasn't saying much. She was also the most annoying, insisting on using her navy-blue Yale coffee mug for breakfast, as if she had to show off her pedigree. I mean, she was in her mid-forties and college was a long time ago. I figured she probably handled the legal aspects of the business. Her husband, Henry, sat quietly beside her as always. I got the impression that Henry only spoke when Carla gave him the okay.

"I do not. That's Paula," Bob said.

Paula took offense. "I don't have a suspicious *passht*. My *passht* is wide open. You should be looking at Arlene when talking about a suspicious *passht*." She eyed her sister-in-law. I didn't like the way Arlene was clutching her knife as she glared back at Paula.

"Children!" Doris tapped her spoon on her glass. "Quiet! Can't we all just get along for one week?"

Silence ensued while they all got busy with their food. Arlene primly rearranged the napkin in her lap while still managing to shoot daggers at Paula. Even Ed's hammering had stopped, which was kind of weird. Maybe he was taking a break. I should see if he wanted some breakfast.

Carla broke the silence. "Did you take the last pancake?" She jerked her head toward Bob's plate.

Bob shoved a maple-syrup-soaked piece of pancake into his mouth and gestured toward the buffet and its empty silver pancake platter. "No one's name was on it. Maybe you should fill your plate once instead of taking little bits and going up four times."

Carla folded her arms across her chest. "I was going up for seconds. You always take the last pancake. It's not fair." She turned to her mother. "Right?"

Doris rolled her eyes again.

Merow!

"What was that?" Bob made a show of looking around the room, probably hoping to change the subject. "Is that one of those adorable cats you have here?"

Adorable? I supposed they were sort of cute when they weren't pushing things off the counter or ripping the toilet paper off the roll... or finding dead bodies.

"Yes." I glanced at the door to the hallway. The meow sounded far away, like it had come from the closed-off west wing where Ed's hammering had been. It also sounded eerily like the meows they'd made a few weeks ago when they were trying to alert us that a guest was dead in that very same wing. I glanced around the table. Nope, all guests accounted for, thankfully.

"Don't try to change the subject." Carla stabbed her fork into a piece of pancake on Bob's plate.

"Hey!" Bob took his knife and tried to knock the pancake off Carla's fork.

You'd think they were ten years old and not grown adults with children of their own. Thankfully they hadn't brought any of them. I could only imagine what *those* kids were like.

Meoooo! This one was louder and more insistent.

Doris frowned and craned her neck to look out into the hallway from where the meows were emitting.

"I hate when he takes the last pancake," Paula slurred and listed in her chair.

"Taking the last pancake is nothing compared to some of the things I've seen you people do," Bob said.

Merow! Even louder.

I strained to hear. Was that Ed hammering again? It sounded like he was using the sledgehammer on something, but at least that indicated he was alive. Of course, it was silly of me to assume that every time the cats yowled like that there would be a dead body. But still...

Earl leaned forward, getting into Bob's face. He was blissfully oblivious to the potential hidden meaning of the caterwauling. "What are you talking about?"

Bob shoved another piece of pancake in. "I think you know."

Meroogh!

"What is with those cats?" Doris asked, ignoring the ridiculous pancake argument.

"I'm not sure. They might be hungry." Yeah, that was probably it. Even though it sounded like they were in the west wing, they were probably near their food bowls in the kitchen. Sound tended to get distorted and carry from strange places in this old house. I started in that direction when . . . .

Crash!

That came from the west wing.

Mewooo!

Mewargh!

"Josie!" Ed's voice, loud but shaky, echoed through the house. "You'd better come see this."

Chapter Two

"You stay here and enjoy your breakfast. I'm sure it's nothing. Ed tends to get overly excited," I reassured my guests, who were all staring at me.

I dashed off toward the west wing. Judging by the thunder of footsteps behind me, they didn't stay put as I'd suggested. Darn it! The last thing I needed was some sort of disaster to make them want to check out of the guesthouse early with an unpaid bill. My mind reeled. What could it be? Was it the mold? I'd been told one of the walls was rotting and likely had mold inside. That might put guests off, even though I was fixing it. Maybe it was something else. Ed could have been hurt. Or the cats. Though judging by their meows no damage had been done to their vocal cords.

I really didn't want the Biddefords to follow me, but they seemed determined. And besides, I would just have to go back in the dining room and explain whatever it was that Ed was yelling about to them anyway. I forged ahead full speed with the whole family on my heels. As I reached the door I glanced over my shoulder. Doris was right behind me. Who knew the old girl could run so fast?

Of course, the door to the west wing was locked, just as I'd been instructed by our new building inspector to do, so I had to detour into the kitchen and grab the key out of the drawer. When I came back, I had to clear the Biddefords away from the door to open it. Doris had been bent down peeking through the keyhole.

I unlocked the door, and it swung open. My gaze went immediately to the stairway on the right. That's where the body had been just a few weeks ago. Today, though, there was only some dust. I breathed a sigh of relief.

Merooo! Nero ran over to me and then trotted back to the doorway that led to the room where Ed was. He stopped and looked over his shoulder as if waiting for me to follow. All sounds of hammering and sawing had stopped.

"Ed, are you okay?" I yelled. Ed was elderly, maybe he'd had a heart attack or something.

"I'm fine but I don't think this guy is..."

This guy? I steeled myself as I entered the other room.

The room Ed was working in had been a ballroom at one time. It wasn't gigantic but it wasn't tiny either. It was in quite a state of disrepair; water-stained ceiling, wallpaper coming off in strips. Remnants of the original black-and-white marble-tile flooring were chipped and cracked, and most of the windows were boarded up. I was planning on turning it into a game room. Ed had been replacing the old plaster walls first since we already knew there was water damage.

He was standing in front of the worst damaged section of the wall. He'd made good progress and a large section of the old horsehair plaster had been removed to reveal the inside of the wall. The demolition had created a dusty pile of rubble, and I could see the slats inside the wall. Too bad I could also see something else. A skeleton.

A human skeleton.

"Talk about skeletons in your closet." Bob came up beside me and leaned forward to peer at the bones.

Human bones didn't faze me in the least. I'd been in the middle of training as a medical examiner before giving up my career to raise a family. I immediately took note of the appearance of the bones. They looked dry, brittle. No tendons or flesh stuck to them. The skeleton had been in there for a long time. What was it doing inside the wall? Had it been buried in the wall when the place was built or put in sometime later? And why had no one noticed? Seems like a dead body would have smelled, unless already a skeleton when it was shoved in there.

Paula dug a nip out of her purse and I recognized the black-and-white label of Jack Daniel's. Guess discovering a skeleton called for the hard stuff.

"This calls for a drink!" She downed it in one quick swig to the disapproving glare of her siblings.

Doris didn't admonish Paula. She was busy staring at the skeleton. Her face was pinched, her eyes narrowed. She swayed a bit and I was worried she might faint, but it turned out she was just trying to get a closer look. Before I knew it, she was crouched down beside the skeleton, lifting up its hand. It was wearing a ring—gold with an oval carnelian signet.

"Lordy! It's Jedediah Biddeford! He's come back

to enact the curse just like he said he would!" Doris dropped the hand and the bones clattered as she shot up to a standing position.

Ed raised his brows at me.

The cats sniffed the ring.

"Wait a minute! What curse?" Arlene's gaze shifted between Doris, Earl and the skeleton.

"You didn't tell her about the curse?" Doris shot a look at Earl.

Earl shrugged. "It's just a stupid old wives' tale."

Carla gestured toward the skeleton. "Apparently not. I mean he *is* here."

Earl scowled. "He is not *here*. That's just a skeleton. It's not like it's his ghost or anything." He turned to his wife. "There's an old family legend about an ancestor who will come back and haunt anyone who digs up his treasure."

Carla frowned. "Hey, wait. Does that mean someone dug up treasure?"

Doris's dark eyes scanned the faces of her children. "Well, did anyone?"

They shook their heads.

"I doubt there is an actual treasure..." Bob said slowly. He looked distracted, as if he was wondering if there really was a treasure and, if so, where it might be.

"We don't even know that this is Jedediah," I said. I'd heard about the curse from Millie. Millie's family had bought the guesthouse from Jedediah's family back in the day. Apparently old Jedediah Biddeford had issued some curse meant to warn anyone away from the treasure he was planning on bringing back from

Europe. He claimed he'd come back and haunt whoever messed with his treasure.

"That's his ring." Doris pointed toward the hand. "I
saw an old picture of it once. My granddaddy said Jed
always wore it. Never took it off."

"But Jedediah never came back from Europe. So
that can't possibly be him in there." At least that's what
I'd been told.

Doris looked at me like I had five heads. "Don't
you know? He always said he'd return. And this is the
form he's taken. And if he's back you know what that
means?" She looked around at her kids like a lady who
was sure she had the winning lottery ticket. "The treasure came back too."

"I'll drink to that!" Paula had dug out another nip.
She raised the Jack Daniel's in the air then threw her
head back and chugged it down.

Ed scowled at Doris. "Lady. This isn't a ghost. This
is a skeleton. He hasn't come back." Ed poked at the
femur bone with a long old-fashioned oak folding ruler.
"This guy's been in here for a couple hundred years."

"What the—"

I turned to see the guesthouse maid, Flora, in the
doorway. Flora had sort of come with the place. Millie
had assured me she did a great job. At what, I had no
idea because for most of the tasks I gave her, she simply claimed she didn't "do" that sort of work. I did see
her dusting sometimes, but mostly she could be found
watching the new TV in the parlor. She must have
been on a commercial break and come to check out the
ruckus.

Flora was a tiny thing with a shock of white hair and round glasses that made her eyes look gigantic. I had no idea how old Flora was but if I had to guess I'd say she was about as old as the guesthouse itself. Probably knew Jedediah Biddeford personally.

She narrowed her gaze at the skeleton. "What's that?"

"Jedediah Biddeford," Doris said.

Flora's brows shot up. "You mean the guy who buried the treasure? He really did come back from Europe?"

Great. Even Flora believed in the curse. That's all I needed, a bunch of treasure hunters digging up the place.

Doris nodded. "Yep."

"I doubt it's him," Ed reiterated.

"Did he really bury treasure?" Henry seemed interested in something for the first time since he'd arrived.

"Doubt it." Earl didn't sound convinced.

"Stranger things have happened." Paula leaned against the wall, probably to keep from falling down.

"It's nonsense," Ed said, waving his hand dismissively. "Old rumors probably got all misconstrued over the years. I'd be more concerned about how the guy got here. Someone stuffed him in and closed up the wall. That's no curse. That's murder."

The room fell silent as we all let Ed's words sink in.

Flora broke the silence. "I don't know who he is, if he buried treasure or who put him in there, but I do know that I'm not cleaning this mess up. I don't do skeletons." She gave me a pointed look and then turned and shuffled off toward the hallway.

Ed had a point. Whoever the skeleton was, he didn't get into that wall on his own. And while I didn't believe in curses and I was darn sure there was no treasure buried at the guesthouse, I did know one thing. This discovery was a police matter.

I dug my phone out of my pocket and dialed the sheriff.

*

Nero sat off to the side, preening his sleek black fur as he watched the humans inspect the skeleton. Of course, he and Marlowe had known the skeleton was in the wall for quite some time now, but Josie hadn't heeded the many warnings they'd given her.

"If only she'd listened to us two weeks ago when we were trying to alert her by scratching on the wallpaper. Then she wouldn't have made the guests aware of this gruesome discovery." Marlowe's mottled black-and-ginger tail swished on the floor, clearing away a swath of dust.

"Indeed. Her communication skills are not progressing as quickly as they should."

Nero glanced at Josie. They'd inherited the tall redhead when Millie had put them in charge of the guesthouse. Oh sure, it was all disguised as a sale of the property and Millie had told Josie she couldn't have cats at the senior housing where she was moving and that their continued presence at the guesthouse was a condition of the sale.

But Nero knew the truth. Millie was getting on in years and wanted to enjoy life free from the responsibility of running a business. She still loved her precious Oyster Cove Guesthouse and had left the most trustworthy being on the planet in charge—Nero. Of course, Marlowe thought that she was also in charge, but Nero knew the responsibility lay mostly with him. Marlowe was, after all, Nero's protégée and therefore a subordinate. Lord knew Marlowe had a lot to learn, not the least of which was how to investigate a murder properly. At the rate the younger cat was progressing, Nero feared it might be two lifetimes before she came up to speed.

Still, it didn't hurt to let Marlowe think she was more important than she was and on equal footing in guesthouse responsibilities. Sometimes one had to let others think things were one way, even when you knew the real truth. Like the fact that Josie thought she was in control of the guesthouse simply because Millie had sold her the property, for example. Silly humans.

Though much superior, Nero had to admit cats couldn't do everything that humans could, so naturally they needed Josie as a frontwoman to run things. Nero also had no desire to concern himself with the more mundane tasks of cooking, laundry, accounting and the like. That's what humans were for.

Unfortunately, Josie had proven to be a slow learner. She didn't listen to them like Millie did. And that's why she had misunderstood their previous communication about what was inside the wall, thinking it was merely mold or dry rot. Oh well, she would learn eventually. He hoped.

Marlowe grimaced as the old lady, Doris Biddeford,

picked up the skeleton's hand and let it fall back. "That's tampering with a crime scene."

Nero smiled. As the older and wiser cat, he'd been training Marlowe in the ways of a cat detective. Because that's what they were, not merely stewards of the Oyster Cove Guesthouse, but also detectives of the feline variety who helped humans solve their cases. The humans had no inkling of their help, of course. It was quite a trick to point them toward clues and reveal suspects, all the while making them think it was their idea.

"It is of little matter. There will not be much to investigate here," Nero said.

Marlowe jerked her gaze toward the skeleton, her face scrunched in disappointment. "What do you mean? There's a body inside the wall. That guy didn't get there on his own, just like Ed said."

"That much is true, but this death doesn't warrant a feline investigation. It doesn't take a forensic anthropologist to see the skeleton has been in there for centuries." Nero jerked his head toward the skeleton. "I mean look at it, it's all dried out and smells of old hatred and long-buried criminal intent."

"I suppose you're right."

Nero nodded sagely. He usually was right, at least when it came to matters of murder. "What would there be to investigate? The killer is long dead. No suspects to follow or clues to unearth."

"Wouldn't be much fun, I guess." Marlowe's disappointment was palpable. Good girl. At least someone here was progressing nicely. Marlowe had made great strides during the last investigation and now wanted to try her hand at another, and that was a good sign. But just not *this* investigation, because there was simply nothing to explore.

Nero loved nothing more than to sink his claws into a juicy murder, but this death was about as interesting as a week-old can of sardines. "Besides, much of the satisfaction is bringing the killer to justice and this killer is long gone already."

Marlowe yawned and stretched out her front paws. "I just wish there was *something* for us to investigate."

Nero didn't want to get Marlowe's hopes up, but if his seventh sense was as good as it usually was, there *was* something going on inside the guesthouse that may need investigation soon. He couldn't quite put his finger on it, but he'd sensed little undercurrents, sneaky nefarious vibrations. Unfortunately, very soon, Marlowe might get her wish.

"Odd, none of the guests seem disturbed by this discovery." Nero studied their faces and posture. He could tell they were interested in the skeleton but not in a who-killed-my-ancestor kind of way. He could also tell that they were all trying to conceal their interest from each other.

"They seem more excited than anything," Marlowe said.

"They are an odd bunch. Don't seem to like each other much."

Marlowe's green eyes narrowed to luminescent slits. "No. And I think they have secrets."

Nero's whiskers twitched. So Marlowe *had* noticed the whispers and secret meetings. Good for her.

"I'm not sure any of them can be trusted," Nero warned. "Though their business sounds delightful. All that cheese."

"Odd business, isn't it? Cheese sculptures? Wouldn't think there would be a big call for it among humans."

"Maybe that's why they are not doing well." Nero sniffed the air. His keen olfactory senses had been flooded with the scents of Brie and cheddar since the new guests had arrived. It was enough to drive a cat mad. "Though I think their business not doing well is due more to infighting."

"You'll get no argument from me there. I don't know how Josie stands it with them constantly snapping at each other," Marlowe said.

"I think Josie is just happy to have paying guests. At least that's how I'd look at it," Nero said. "She's practical and that's a good way to be. Now if only we could get her to actually pay attention to us."

"Do you think we've been too soft on her?"

Nero thought about it for a second. There was a fine line between creating a bond with your human and spoiling them to the point where they thought they were in control. "I've been taking her seat every night in the chair she loves to sit in in the parlor. You know, the overstuffed comfy one that shows off the black hairs I shed?"

"Yeah, and I've been lying on her keyboard when she wants to type, then sticking my tail in her face when she tries to move me."

"And we've been going into the dining room when the guests are in there eating, just like she asked us not to." Nero glanced up at Josie. She did seem to be taking command of the situation. At least she wasn't swooning or acting all weirded out about the skeleton. "Maybe we are expecting progress too quickly. I mean, she did finally get our drift about the murder a few weeks ago."

"Yes, that is something at least." Marlowe threaded her way through Doris Biddeford's ankles. "Do you think there really is treasure out there somewhere?"

Nero's whiskers twitched at the mention of treasure. Oh, how fun that would be. His claws itched to grab onto some dirt and really dig. But if there had been treasure on the grounds, surely his superior senses would have alerted him long ago. "Doubtful. Though by the looks of the humans, they might believe in such a thing."

Marlowe finished her route around the humans' ankles and trotted back to where Nero was under the window. "Come on, let's go claw some dirt out of those plants in the conservatory. Millie brought them even though Josie hasn't had Ed finish the room yet and no one will even notice we've been near them. I'm in the mood for digging."

"Perfect. Josie won't like that at all." Nero stood and stretched.

"Yes, one more way to show her she doesn't own us."

"Good thinking." Josie had made the mistake of saying that once and it really stuck in Nero's craw. Apparently, Marlowe felt the same.

"I just hope Josie doesn't withhold treats once she discovers the mess," Marlowe said as she led the way out.

Nero paused at the doorway and looked over his

shoulder at the Biddefords, who were talking animatedly while Josie called the cops on her cell phone. "Me either. But somehow I have the feeling a little dirt and an old skeleton are going to be the least of Josie's problems."

Chapter Three

"Who says he never made it back from Europe? Maybe this happened when he got back from Europe," Mom whispered to Millie and me in the hall after the sheriff, Seth, had kicked us out of the room.

Millie nodded. "Good point, Rose. But either way, whoever did it is long gone. Still, maybe we could do some research and come up with a list of possible suspects."

"Might not be very much fun, though, if we can't confront the culprit and see him arrested," Mom said as she and Millie slowed to a crawl. Apparently, they couldn't walk fast while their minds were full of the possibility of a new investigation.

I sped ahead and continued down the hallway. The Biddefords had all disappeared and I felt it was my duty to make sure they weren't shaken by these new events. Whoever was in the wall was likely a relative...or had been murdered by one.

I heard a murmur of conversation from the dining room and headed in that direction. The Biddefords were there, but they weren't sitting in shocked silence contemplating their lost ancestor as I'd imagined. They were scarfing up the remains of the breakfast. There were no sniffles, or muted grieving tones. The room was abuzz with excitement.

"I'll tell you exactly what this means," Doris said. "This means that Jedediah really did bury that treasure."

"I thought the curse was that he would come back to enact some revenge on anyone who messed with his treasure. Doesn't seem like he came back to me. Looks like he'd been there the whole time." Paula strolled along the server looking at what was left of breakfast. She stopped in front of the pumpkin bread and my heart leapt. Would she cut a piece? I wondered if the excessive drinking had dulled her palate. Then again, that might be a good thing if she was going to eat my pumpkin bread.

Doris pinched off a piece of bacon and fed it to Nero, who was skulking around under the table. Darn cat, I'd told him not to go in the dining room when guests were eating. They never listened. I was sure Marlowe wasn't far behind either. Yep, her tail was sticking out from under Earl's chair.

"Nonsense! You know how those old curses are, they get all mixed up because they're handed down generation to generation. It's like that game where you whisper in each other's ears and by the time it gets to the end, it's not even close to what it was when it started. The specifics of the curse might have been different too. But there's one thing for sure. He did come back—seeing as his skeleton was found in the wall," Doris said.

Her children looked at her with a mixture of doubt and greed in their eyes.

Paula picked up a knife, her hand hovering over the loaf. I held my breath.

"Did anyone try a piece of this?" Paula bent down and sniffed. She eyed the loaf as if it were trying to trick her, then put the knife down.

No one answered her.

"Maybe I'll just have some more eggs." She scooped some onto a plate and returned to her seat.

"But now what does it mean? If he came back doesn't that mean someone took his treasure? And how, exactly, will he get revenge?" Arlene asked.

"Maybe the opening of the wall has released his ghost," Henry answered, eyes scanning the edges of the room, no doubt looking for Jed's spirit. Would tourists want to stay in a haunted guesthouse or was that off-putting to most? Hopefully this would all be cleared up before word got out and I had to find out firsthand if having a ghost would be bad for business.

Mom and Millie had come in behind me, but the Biddefords were too engrossed in their conversation to notice us.

"If someone did take his treasure, that person is long dead, so good luck to old Jed for getting his revenge." Earl popped a grape into his mouth.

"How do you know he even made it to Europe?" Arlene asked.

"He must have, because I remember seeing family letters he sent from overseas." Bob poured a cup of coffee and slurped.

"But what about those rumors that he never came back? Wouldn't people have noticed that he did?" Carla asked.

"I know!" Doris fed a scrap of bacon to Marlowe this

time. "I bet you he kept it a secret because he had the treasure. He didn't want anyone to know he was back because he wanted time to bury it."

"But then someone came in and bashed him over the head and buried *him* in the wall!" Bob sounded almost gleeful.

"Yeah, but the question is, did he bury the treasure first or did the killer get it?" Paula asked.

Her question was met with silence as they contemplated this.

"I bet he buried it first. If he hadn't buried it, then surely the family records would have shown someone spending a lot of money." Earl turned to Doris. "There weren't any rumors about a big influx of money back during that time, were there?"

Doris pressed her lips together. "Well, that was a bit before my time, but I don't remember anything about sudden wealth. If someone found it, they could have doled it out a little bit at a time. The family originally had a lot of money from Jed's spice import business, but since future generations had to sell off the house, I'm gonna assume there was no treasure chest of riches found."

Paula's eyes lit up. "It could still be buried here."

"Yeah, but where?" Bob glanced out the window.

"Maybe he didn't bury it, maybe he hid it in the house somewhere?" Henry said.

Doris scowled at him as if he were dense. "I hope not. Most of the original structure from Jed's time—aside from that one ballroom wall where he has been found—has been torn down and renovated. I remember my grandfather showing me that the only part that hadn't been touched from the old house was that wall where Jed's skeleton was. And there was no treasure in the wall with him, so if it was hidden somewhere else in the house someone would have found it by now."

"Mom's right," Earl said. "Besides, I think I remember the curse having something to do with haunting anyone who *dug up* the treasure—he must have intended to bury it. Our best bet is to look on the grounds."

"So my question still stands, *where* on the grounds?" Bob said.

"I wonder if he left a map?" Arlene asked.

Earl put his arm around her. "That's a good question, honey. You're always thinking. Where would he have left it?"

"Hopefully not hidden in the house; otherwise that's gone too," Doris said.

"Maybe he had it on him?" Paula suggested.

"In the wall?" Earl glanced toward the hallway. "We should go look."

"Can't," Doris said. "The police are in there now. Besides, I looked in there pretty good and didn't see anything but that ring and a bunch of bones. We all got there together so no one would have had time to take the map out without the rest of us seeing them do it."

"Can we look in any of the family documents?" Bob asked Doris. "Did Grandpa Biddeford ever mention anything about a map?"

"He never mentioned anything to me." Doris waved her hands. "You can look if you want. I'm not gonna waste my time looking for some map."

"What if someone did find out and never said anything." Carla tapped her fork on her empty plate. "There might not even be any treasure."

"True, but what if it wasn't found…then it could still be out there." Doris gestured toward the window.

"Don't any of you care who killed him?" I asked. I'd walked to the buffet and was bravely cutting into the pumpkin bread. One didn't have to be a master chef to see it was a little dry. I'd have to work on that recipe, but for now copious amounts of butter should make it palatable.

The conversation stopped and they all looked at me, then at each other. Doris shook her head.

"Nah! None of us knew him and, besides, the killer is long dead. Whoever did it got what's coming to him. That's old news. What's *new* news is the treasure, and I'm fixin' to be the one who digs it up, my business depends on it!" She pushed up from the table and hurried out of the room.

"Hey, where's she going?" Arlene asked.

Earl leaped from his chair and pulled Arlene up with him. "My guess is to scout out likely spots."

Bob threw down his napkin and followed them out of the room.

Carla jumped up. "Come on, Henry. We're not letting them get a head start!"

Paula remained seated at the table alone. She looked shell-shocked. After a few beats, she stumbled up from the chair and spun in the direction of the door. "Hey, wait for me!"

Meow.

Marlowe and Nero were at my feet looking up at me, probably waiting for a crumb of pumpkin bread to fall. Unlike most cats, these two would eat anything.

"Yeah, sure, now that everyone is gone, you're looking to me for food? I thought I told you two not to come in here when the guests were eating."

Millie scooped Nero up in her arms.

"See, they never listen to me." I examined the piece of pumpkin bread in my hand. I'd put so much butter on it, it looked like frosting. Surely something with that much butter couldn't taste bad.

"Now, dear," Millie clucked. "Cats have their own rules. You have to listen to *them* not the other way around." She picked a dried leaf from Nero's fur. "Have they been digging in the plants? Naughty. Naughty."

Nero purred and rubbed his cheek against Millie's while casting a see-that's-how-you-treat-me look in my direction.

I took a tentative bite. Just as I suspected, it was dry and tasted like sawdust.

"Josie, I hope you've been watering those plants." Millie put Nero down and picked up Marlowe.

"I have," I managed to choke out while trying to swallow the pumpkin bread. Truthfully, I'd forgotten about the gigantic potted trees that Millie had bought at a yard sale last week. She said they'd go perfectly in the conservatory, which they would have if the room was anywhere near being done. Right now it was as dilapidated as the ballroom. I didn't want to look a gift horse in the mouth so I accepted them and put them in the room near one of the windows that wasn't boarded up. Hopefully they weren't as dried up and dead as the skeleton.

Millie looked at the piece of pumpkin bread in my hand. "Is that what you're making for the town celebration?" She must have noticed I was trying, unsuccessfully, to choke down that one little bite.

"It was a recipe I tried. It needs some work," I admitted.

"Looks dry. Maybe add some more oil." Millie was a whiz at baking. She'd generously left her recipes here when I'd bought the guesthouse. Lucky thing for me she also kept popping in to bake too. If it wasn't for Millie the guests might have starved. Though I was a tad bit insulted she thought I couldn't handle the cooking, I had to admit she was right.

"I can help you on that later." Millie glanced toward the hallway. "Once the police are done. Hopefully Mike will tell us what they said."

"Mike?" I picked a crumb off the pumpkin bread and dropped it on my tongue. Even that was dry. "I thought he left. I mean, doesn't he have building-inspector business to tend to?"

Mom and Millie exchanged a look.

"So, you are interested!" Millie sounded as if she'd just won the lottery.

"No," I said. "I just thought he had left."

"He's in the crime-scene room making sure Seth doesn't damage anything," Millie said.

That figured. I was willing to bet Mike was hanging around for more reasons than to make sure nothing got damaged. He'd been an investigator in the navy and, judging by his actions when we'd found the last body, he still couldn't resist an investigation. How he'd ended up a handyman turned building inspector was anyone's guess. He'd told me it was because he liked to work with his hands, though I suspected at the time that *that* statement had a double meaning.

Thoughts of the last investigation reminded me of how annoying Mike could be. He'd insinuated that I had no business investigating to clear my own name and practically ordered me to stop looking for the killer. The nerve!

Good thing I had no interest in getting to the bottom of this skeleton case. He could have it.

"If you thought he left, you must have been thinking of him," Mom said in that tone that indicated she knew my mind better than I did. "I don't blame you. He's a hottie. And he's a very nice boy."

"Just because you made a bad choice for your last husband doesn't mean you can't try again," Millie added.

My "bad choice" was the other reason I'd come back to Oyster Cove. No wonder I was no good at cooking. My ex-husband was a semi-famous chef, so naturally he'd done all the cooking when we were married. He'd also done a lot of other things that I won't bore you with. The divorce was not amicable and the only good thing that came from that marriage was my daughter, Emma. It had all turned out for the best, though. I was finding a new freedom and, by running the guesthouse, learning I was capable and self-sufficient. I didn't need anyone to take care of me or tell me what to do, especially not Mike Sullivan.

"What do you make of all this Jedediah Biddeford business?" I changed the subject.

"*Notsh oroamnl oar*," my mom mumbled. While we'd been talking about my love life, she'd grabbed a plate and helped herself to the buffet.

"Huh?"

"She said she's not sure she believes in the curse," Millie translated.

"Yeah, me either," I said. "But still there *is* a skeleton in the wall."

"Right. And that means shenanigans," Millie said.

Mom washed down her bacon with a swig of juice. "He must have been killed for a reason."

"Maybe nothing to do with treasure, though," I said.

"Of course, the mere notion of treasure here on the property is ridiculous," Millie said softly as she cast a wistful glance out the window.

"If there was one, I'm sure we'd have heard about it by now." I tossed the rest of my pumpkin bread onto one of the dishes and started clearing the table.

"Or someone would have dug it up. Right, Rose?" Millie asked my mother.

"Right." Mom stuffed the last bit of food in her mouth and headed toward the door. "But just the same, I want to be prepared."

"Where are you going?" I stacked more dirty dishes on top of each other.

"Why, down to Ace Hardware to buy a shovel, of course," Mom called over her shoulder. "Hurry, Millie. A little digging will be good exercise and you never know what we might find!"

Chapter Four

Nero stretched out in the puddle of sunshine on the conservatory floor. The guesthouse was blissfully silent; all the guests had gone out to buy shovels and Josie had gone to the store. He rolled this way and that, enjoying the warmth on his fur and smelling the fresh scent of the dirt from the plants. He stretched his claws, noting that there was still a smidge of dirt under the nails from digging in the enormous pot of the ficus tree that sat next to the window. Sure, they could dig all they wanted outside, but there was nothing like digging up a plant in the comfort of your own home. Plus, it would help keep Josie on her toes, and impress upon her that cats didn't simply obey human orders.

The conservatory faced east and therefore had a delightful view of Smugglers Bay, with its craggy rock inlet and sun-dappled waves. Too bad most of the conservatory windows were boarded up. The room would have a magnificent view once new ones were installed.

Nero didn't mind the windows on the far side of the room being boarded as those blocked the view of the neighboring Smugglers Bay Inn. Not only was that inn somewhat of a rival to the guesthouse, but the owner, Stella Dumont, and Josie were rivals for the affections of Mike Sullivan. Even if Josie herself didn't realize this yet, Nero was firmly on Josie's side. The less he had to look at Smugglers Bay Inn *and* Stella Dumont, the better.

From his spot, he could just see the edge of the deck where Stella served meals. He watched the gulls swooping in circles above it. There were more there now than there had been last week, and he was glad their numbers were no longer diminishing, even though they insisted on tormenting the cats by dive-bombing them.

Of course, Nero himself was not afraid of the gulls. Those times he ducked under a hydrangea when a gull swooped were only to demonstrate to the other cats what they could do to protect themselves...even if no cats were around to see.

"The gulls are in good form today, I see," said Marlowe, her luminescent green eyes following Nero's gaze.

"Let's hope they discourage some of the diners at the Smugglers Bay Inn." Nero figured anything that drove customers away from the inn was good for the guesthouse.

"It's nice and quiet in here now with all the guests gone." Marlowe trotted to another small patch of sun in the corner and curled into a tight ball, wrapping her tail around her nose.

"Silly of them to run off after shovels, don't you think?" Nero asked.

Marlowe raised her head. "I suppose so. Humans are always looking for some sort of treasure when all they really need to make life worth living is free. What would they do with it anyway? Probably just spend it on silly material things."

Nero nodded sagely. "Humans just don't get it like we do. All we need is a warm meal and a comfortable spot in the sun. Though I do enjoy the gravy cat food and manufactured treats that Josie buys from the store."

Nero heard a commotion in the foyer.

"Looks like the blissful silence is over. Someone is home." Marlowe sighed.

Nero's ears perked up, listening to discover who it was. He couldn't quite hear what was being said, but he sensed it was the two brothers, Bob and Earl. His whiskers tingled. Something was going on between them and he was sure it was not good. He stood and stretched.

"I think we should take a trot upstairs and see what these humans are up to."

Marlowe slit one eye open, obviously reluctant to leave her sunny spot. "You think they're up to something? I have noticed a certain amount of strain between the siblings. Not to mention a tinge of animosity and nefarious thoughts."

"Indeed. Perhaps this treasure will bind them together." Nero gestured toward the doorway. Marlowe could be a bit lazy, but skulking around and finding out what the humans were up to was important cat business.

"Or set them at each other's throats even more." Marlowe rose, stretching so hard that her back cracked.

"Let's take the back stairs. I hear them up near their rooms."

The mansion had several sets of stairs, but the back stairs near the kitchen were Nero's favorite. The old narrow treads that creaked under human weight were silent when cats ran up them, allowing Nero and Marlowe to sneak around the mansion without being heard. They were covered in layers of white paint so thick that it was almost soft. No human liked to go in the confined space, which made it even more perfect for cats. He and Marlowe trotted up stealthily, spilling out into the jewel-toned oriental runner that ran the length of the second-story hallway where most of the habitable rooms were situated.

Nero was surprised to see Flora standing in the middle of the hallway with a pink feather duster in her hand. She was dusting off a credenza on which sat various knick-knacks that Nero liked to push to the floor every so often. Her head was bent about two inches from the surface so that she could inspect her own work. Poor Flora—even with her coke-bottle glasses, her eyesight wasn't the best.

Marlowe and Nero exchanged a glance. They'd never seen her so intent on cleaning. Was Flora turning over a new leaf?

They skulked along the perimeter of the hallway, ears cocked and superior hearing senses on alert to overhear what the humans were saying. Nero was a little worried. He'd already suspected the humans were not enamored with each other and now he was concerned the thought of this treasure might cause them to do something crazy. The last thing the guesthouse needed was another scandal. But if such a thing happened, he wasn't going to fall down on the job like he did last time.

"They're each in their rooms," Marlowe whispered, aiming her ears first toward Earl's room and then toward Bob's. "It's boring when they are quiet."

No sooner were the words out of Marlowe's mouth than Bob's door flew open. He stormed over to Earl's room, knocking loudly before being let in.

Marlowe turned and looked at Nero, the whiskers over her left eye sticking up slightly. They both glanced at Flora, who hadn't noticed. She moved on to dusting a plinth that held a marble bust outside of Earl's room.

Yelling drifted from inside the room. The two men were arguing. Nero strained to listen, and Marlowe followed suit. But the arguing had stopped.

Flora continued dusting. She probably couldn't hear them since Nero was sure she was also hard of hearing.

Nero pressed closer to the door. He could hear hushed tones, but he couldn't make out the whole conversation, only snatches.

"...secret book!..."

"...reveal to the rest of them..."

Reveal what? Something in the secret book? Something to do with the treasure?

The door flew open.

Flora jumped back, dropping the duster.

The cats scattered.

Bob stormed out, slammed the door shut and continued to his room.

Flora scowled at him, then shrugged, picked up her feather duster and kept dusting.

Nero sat on his haunches and washed behind his ears. Apparently the Biddefords were already in deep competition for the alleged treasure, and judging by the way he'd seen them fight over pancakes, they might not be willing to share.

Chapter Five

The kitchen of the Oyster Cove Guesthouse held a lot of fond childhood memories. Mom had brought me here often when I was a kid and Millie always had a fresh baked treat for me. Now it was my turn to carry on those delicious recipes. It was a daunting task since everything I tried to bake either came out dry, burned or tasting like dirt.

The kitchen was a mixture of old antique fixtures, cheery yellow-painted cabinets and newer stainless-steel appliances. The worn, wide, pine flooring creaked in all the right places and the space always had the savory, sweet smell of family-style cooking. At least it had when Millie owned it. Now it mostly smelled like a two-alarm fire.

I'd just returned from picking up some supplies and was riffling through the yellowed, grease-smudged recipes trying to pick out another type of sweet bread since the pumpkin hadn't worked out so well, when I glanced out the window to see Stella Dumont on the deck of the Smugglers Bay Inn looking toward my place.

Yes, *that* Stella Dumont. The one Mike had dumped me for in high school. Not that that had anything to do with the urge I had to trip her every time I saw her. Those feelings were more to do with her acting superior about her inn, as if it was more desirable than mine. Sure, hers was closer to the ocean with that deck overlooking the water, but at least I didn't have seagulls pooping all over my guests' food.

Her inn was pretty far from my place, separated by a large field that gently sloped downward. My guesthouse was situated atop the hill and had a nice panoramic view of Smugglers Bay and the Atlantic Ocean. Some said it was a much better view than Stella's inn had and I agreed.

I kind of had to squint to make out who the scrawny figure on the deck was, but I was pretty sure it was her. Why was she looking in this direction? It looked as if she was scoping out the property. Of course, she could be looking for Mike. She'd been known to pop over here a time or two to try to talk to him while he was still working here, finishing up the renovations Millie had hired him to do before she sold the place. Mike didn't work here anymore, so what was Stella looking for? Had word already gotten around town about Jed's skeleton and the mythical treasure? I hoped she wasn't looking for potential treasure-hiding spots. Would more people come and try to dig? I was kind of hoping it would all die down and I wouldn't have to figure out how to stop people from churning up the grounds. The Biddefords were my immediate problem. They seemed keen to dig up the treasure but I was sure I'd heard at least two of them come home and no one had started digging yet, so maybe they weren't as keen on putting in the manual labor necessary.

"Seth's done in the west wing and the body has been removed." I jumped at the words, then turned to see Mike lounging in the doorway. His gaze shifted to the window. Was he looking out hoping to see Stella?

"I didn't realize you were still here," I said.

"Yeah, I wanted to make sure that the Sheriff's Department didn't mess with the structural integrity of the wall when they were getting their evidence out," Mike said.

"Oh, I didn't realize that was part of the building inspector's job." Was it? Or was he giving the guest-house special treatment? Of course, if he was giving it special treatment it was probably because his aunt was still attached to it, and not because of me.

"Also, Ed wanted me to double-check on his plan for redoing the conservatory, so we don't run into any code violations later on."

"Oh." I guess maybe he was here officially. I turned back to my recipes.

"So anyway, this treasure thing is kind of interesting, huh?" He'd made his way across the room and was now leaning his hip against the countertop, mere inches from where I stood. "You think there really is a treasure out there?"

"I doubt it. If there was, my mom and Millie would've probably dug it up by now."

Mike laughed. "Yeah, they sure are a pair, aren't they? I heard something about them going downtown for shovels. Probably rushing back already so they can start digging any minute."

I snorted. "No doubt." Millie had requested I meet

them at the town common later that day to go over how I wanted the Oyster Cove Guesthouse display to be set up for the town celebration. She'd said this was of the utmost importance because the display needed to be perfect so that tourists coming for the celebration would be enticed to book a future vacation at the guesthouse, but I wouldn't be surprised if she canceled so she could dig for treasure.

"Are you going to go out and dig?" He leaned in closer.

I sidled away, clutching at the recipe I'd just pulled out. Cranberry-orange bread. I guessed that would do for the celebration. "Nope." I held the recipe in the air between us. "I need to try out this recipe for the town celebration. It's really important I have something to offer that represents the Oyster Cove Guesthouse."

His eyes drifted out the window again in the direction of the Smugglers Bay Inn. My heart twitched. If I kept putting Mike off, I was driving him right toward Stella Dumont. But if he had intentions toward her, I didn't really want him anyway.

He pushed away from the counter. "Well, I gotta get back to the town offices. Let me know if you need anything and don't forget to make sure you get your proper inspections for Ed's work."

He was all business now, probably thinking about what he might like to inspect over at the Smugglers Bay Inn.

"Will do." I watched him leave, glad to have some alone time. I needed to concentrate on the loaf recipe.

As I pawed through the file trying to choose

between the cranberry-orange bread I had in my hand, the apple-pecan bread and the peanut-butter-banana bread, I could hear the Biddefords coming back inside. They were in rare form, jostling and arguing. Not much different from before the discovery of the skeleton, but I'd probably have to lay down the law about digging. I didn't want the yard filled with dangerous holes.

I glanced into the yard just in time to see Henry skulking around the corner of the old chicken coop, near the shed. Now there was an odd one, always with his head buried in a book. He was very quiet and didn't seem to mesh with the rest of the family at all. I'd heard in snippets of conversations that Henry was also one of the most skilled cheese sculptors of the entire clan and had become famous for a very detailed sculpture of the Taj Mahal in white cheddar.

What was he doing out by the shed? The shed was a newer structure and old Jed wouldn't have used it as a landmark for his treasure cache since it wasn't around during his time.

I craned my neck, pressing my face almost to the glass to get a better look. It didn't look like he was digging up anything. He didn't even have a shovel. It almost looked as if he was spying on someone, but I couldn't see who because he was casting furtive glances in my direction. Whoever the person was they were hidden behind the tall, overgrown shrubbery on the other side of the kitchen window.

I rushed to the pantry because the window in there was on the other side of the shrubs. Darn it! I still couldn't see anyone, but I could hear the low murmur of voices.

"Just what do you think you're getting at?"

I recognized Carla's nasal Ivy League twang but she obviously wasn't arguing with Henry. He was on the other side of the yard spying on her.

"You know what I'm getting at..."

Was that Bob? He sounded awfully mean and mad.

"...not gonna stand for it, you make it right or else..." Bob again. *What* wasn't he going to stand for?

"Ha! I don't answer to you." Carla's hushed whisper was sharp with anger.

Unfortunately, they then lowered their voices and I couldn't hear what they were saying. After a few minutes of ear straining, Carla's voice came through once more, loud and clear. "Don't bet on it."

The sound of rustling shrubs and Carla cursing under her breath signaled the end of the conversation. I rushed back to the kitchen, my mind whirling. What in the world was that about? I knew the whole family was at odds but clearly Carla was up to something and Bob was calling her out.

I peeked out the window in time to see Henry walking over to meet Carla. They were about twenty feet from the window now and I could see Carla had two shovels.

"What was that about?" Henry asked.

Carla glanced back toward the shrubbery and I jumped back from the window. Not that I was doing anything wrong, but still...

"Don't worry, I'm not gonna just stand by and take

his crap. This time I'm going to do something about it," she said as she thrust one of the shovels into Henry's hands. As they turned and stalked off, her words rang in my ears. I couldn't shake the fact that her tone was unmistakably threatening.

Chapter Six

Carla's words were still echoing in my head an hour later when I pulled up to the town common where they were setting up for the 250-year celebration. Millie and Mom hadn't canceled or shown up at the guesthouse to dig up the grounds, so I assumed our meeting was still on. It was a perfect day with a cloudless blue sky, warm sun shining down, and birds twittering and flying in the leaves of the stately oaks and maples that lined the common.

The smells of fresh peaches and honeysuckle mingled with the sounds of volunteers hammering the stakes for the giant white tents under which other volunteers were setting up tables for the various town businesses to place their brochures and items for sale. At the far end, a myriad of colorful boats could be seen moored in Oyster Cove, with the sound of the ocean lapping against the town docks and the cry of seagulls in the background.

Under the tents, the area was abuzz with town merchants vying for the best spot for their table. The celebration didn't open to the public for another day, but everyone wanted to make sure everything was perfect.

I found Millie at the front of the tent, draping a

red gingham tablecloth on a long white plastic folding table.

"Hi, Josie, what do you think?" Millie placed some Oyster Cove Guesthouse pamphlets into a plastic holder and stood back to admire her handiwork.

"It looks pretty good," I said.

"You can pile up the baked goods over here, and then I thought we would put that book about the history of the guesthouse over here. You know, the one in the bookcase in the owner's quarters?" She pointed to various spots on the table then turned an inquisitive face toward me. "You *are* nailing down the baked goods, aren't you?"

"Yep. I'm going to do peanut-butter-banana bread." Of all the recipes I'd culled out, that one sounded the most interesting. I mean, who doesn't like peanut butter and bananas? I tried to sound confident but the look on Millie's face made me think I'd missed the mark. Maybe that recipe was above my level.

After a few seconds, she nodded. "A very good choice. If you need help let me know."

My eyes drifted to the next table. To my dismay I spotted a pamphlet for the Smugglers Bay Inn.

"Stella Dumont's display is right next to ours?" My tone was incredulous.

Millie's excited expression soured. "Yes. Can you believe that? I talked to Fay Weinstein from the Chamber of Commerce to try to get it moved, but she wouldn't do it. Two guesthouses advertising next to each other. It's preposterous, isn't it, Rose?" She turned to my mother who simply nodded.

I scrutinized Stella's table. It was decked out in an eyelet-lace tablecloth with crystal candleholders and a pile of magnets and lip balm with the Smugglers Bay Inn logo. If you ask me, her logo of a one-eyed bearded pirate with a parrot on his shoulder was a little clichéd. The Oyster Cove Guesthouse didn't have a logo, but if it did I would pick something a bit more elegant. Maybe I *should* have one, though. Would it make a difference in bookings?

I wondered what Stella was baking. She'd been known to steal recipes from Millie.

"I hear Stella is making a lemon custard," Millie clucked disapprovingly and gestured toward the sky. "I mean with this heat, doesn't she know the custard will sour?"

Hopefully it *would* sour and fewer people would go to her inn and they would come to mine instead.

The buzz of activity behind us continued as we talked. Townspeople rushed around. Merchants came to check their tables and drop things off. There was something odd about the whole thing, though. Most of them had shovels. Had word gotten out about the treasure? Suddenly, I pictured the grounds of the Oyster Cove Guesthouse littered with holes much like the Swiss cheese that the Biddefords used for carving. Visions of lawsuits from people who hurt themselves falling in the holes swam in my mind.

One of the people running around inside the tent was my maid, Flora. Funny, I didn't remember giving her the afternoon off.

Millie noticed me giving her the stink eye.

"Flora is baking for the great-grandmothers of twins' club," she said, as if that explained it.

I remembered Flora boasting about having dozens of grandchildren and a large number of great-grandchildren too. No surprise at least some of them were twins. "What is she making?"

"Chocolate chip, I think." Millie leaned in. "At her age it's hard to get a lot of baking done."

Or maid work. Flora gave us a finger wave. Apparently she was too busy to come over and say hi. Too bad someone else wasn't. Myron Remington.

Myron's family owned the First Oyster Cove Bank and Trust and provided loans for most of the businesses here in town. His family had lived here for generations. I'd gone to school with Myron and he was okay, but he could be a bit snobby. I remembered he'd acted particularly snooty about getting accepted into Yale our senior year. He was wearing his usual designer three-piece suit and high-end Italian leather shoes.

Why was he coming over? He rarely gave me the time of day. Maybe he wanted to talk me into taking out a loan.

"I heard you had a little incident up at the guesthouse," he said.

"Incident?" Millie asked. She could be very defensive about the guesthouse even though she didn't actually own it anymore. "Honestly, it wasn't really an *incident*, just some old history we dug out."

"Well, I don't know if you would call it old history. I heard there was a body inside the wall."

"A skeleton. Been there for a while," Mom said.

"Yeah, that's interesting. Do they know how he got there?" Myron smoothed his red silk paisley tie. He seemed pretty interested in the skeleton. He'd probably heard about the curse, but I doubted he'd be the type to get his hands dirty digging up treasure. Maybe prissy Myron had a ghoulish side that was into skeletons.

"How do you think he got there? A killer put him in there." Mom's blunt reply earned a sharp look from Millie.

Myron blanched. Probably too graphic for his sensibilities. "He? So the skeleton was a male? Do they know who it was, or have any suspects?"

Millie scoffed. "Really, Myron, the guy has been in there for generations. The suspects would all be dead. Kind of hard to investigate that."

I wondered about that. Was Sheriff Chamberlain going to proceed with an investigation? Did he care who the killer was? Did anyone? Anyone that would've known or cared about the victim, be he Jedediah Biddeford or not, was long gone. Even his own descendants didn't seem eager to seek justice for him.

"Is there going to be an investigation?" Myron asked as if reading my thoughts. That concerned me because the last person I wanted to be able to read my thoughts was Myron Remington.

Mom and Millie looked at each other and shrugged.

"Darned if I know," Millie said.

Myron's gaze narrowed. "Well, if anyone would, it would be you, Millie, wouldn't it?"

Millie blushed. "What are you trying to say, Myron?"

"Oh, nothing. Just that you ladies like to investigate." He smoothed down his comb-over. It had started to flap a bit in the breeze. "I heard you were pretty good at it."

Millie's scowl turned into a smile. She straightened and patted her puffy white hair. "Oh, did you really? Isn't that lovely, Rose? Looks like we have a fan."

My mom leaned on her shovel and nodded. She didn't look impressed with having Myron as a fan.

"Though I suppose no investigation would be necessary if it was natural causes," Myron said.

"I don't think it was natural causes, Myron. Who dies of natural causes inside a wall?" Millie asked.

Myron laughed. His laugh wasn't all that pleasant, though. It reminded me of a screeching meerkat. "Right. Good point."

He glanced around, then apparently spotted his next victim a few tables over.

"Well, nice talking to you, ladies. Gotta run." He turned and walked away.

"That Myron never changes, does he?" I turned to see my best friend from high school, Jen Summers. We'd always managed to stay in touch even after I moved away and we both were busy raising our families. I mean, you kind of have to stay in touch with a friend like Jen who knows all your girlhood secrets. One of the highlights about moving back to town had been rekindling my friendship with her.

Besides knowing all my secrets, she was a kind person and a great friend to have. She was also the postmaster in town and, since the post office was the unofficial gathering spot of the Oyster Cove grapevine, she knew all the gossip before anyone else did.

"Hey, they let you out of the post office." I gestured toward the blue post-office uniform she wore. It might have looked industrial on anyone else, but Jen had modified it with a little tuck here and a fancy button there, which gave it a bit of designer flair. Then again, Jen was slim and looked good in most anything—even the butt-end of the cow outfit we'd once worn for Halloween—unlike myself who had a more um... *curvy*... physique.

She gestured toward a table at the back of the tent with a gigantic stamp on it. "I have to set up our table. Don't know why the post office needs to advertise on a table at the town celebration. It's not like you people could go anywhere else for your mail." Jen laughed.

"The post office is very expensive so I get a lot of stuff from UP—" My mom's words were cut off by Millie poking her in the ribs.

Jen pretended like she didn't hear. "Hey, I heard about the skeleton. What's up with that?"

"Ed was working on that old ballroom and found it inside the wall. Kinda creepy, if you ask me," Mom said.

"Well, at least there's no ghost," Jen said. "Is there?"

Her voice held a hopeful tone, but luckily I hadn't seen hide nor hair of any ghost. That was the last thing I needed with all those crazy Biddefords running around. "Nope. No ghost, just a skeleton."

"Some say it's Jedediah Biddeford come back to get his treasure," Jen said.

"Yeah, I've heard that." I glanced around the tent. More people with shovels had shown up. Mom still leaned on hers as if she was protecting it from being stolen right out from under her.

"In fact, it seems like a lot of people are going to be looking to dig it up." Jen looked at Mom's shovel. "I heard the hardware store was sold out of shovels."

"I got one of the last ones," Mom chimed in.

"Lovely. So my yard will be a minefield of holes tomorrow?"

"Is it legal for people to just come on the guesthouse property and dig?" Millie asked. "I mean, it is still private property even if it is a public guesthouse."

"Well, what can you do?" Mom asked. "You can't hire guards to patrol it."

Millie pressed her lips together. "And you want to keep up good relations with the townspeople. Don't want anyone bad-mouthing the guesthouse."

She had a point. If I kicked people off the property they might get angry and take revenge with bad reviews on Yelp. Was there a way I could control the digging and still keep people happy? I wasn't too worried about the yard since the estate had acres, but most of it was run-down. "I'm going to have to lay out some ground rules. Hopefully the whole town won't come out. And hopefully they will get tired of digging when nothing is found the first day."

"What about the Biddefords? They tend to act like they own the place because they used to," Millie said.

"Yeah, they're going to be a tough crowd to control." I said wondering how, exactly, I would control them.

Jen's eyes widened at something over my shoulder and I turned to see Mike making his way toward us. Was the guy everywhere? He swooped over to Millie's side and dropped a kiss on the top of her head.

"Does your job entail inspecting tents too?" I gestured toward the area around us.

Mike smiled, all boyish charm and dimples. "Nice to see you, too, Sunshine."

Jen snorted. Mom and Millie looked pointedly from Mike to me. I pretended to ignore all of them.

"I just came by because I knew Aunt Millie would be here and she said she had something for me."

Millie produced a bag of cookies from her canvas tote bag. "Just baked them this morning."

Odd, usually she came to the kitchen at the guesthouse to bake. Maybe she was getting used to her own kitchen at the independent living resort where she now resided. She'd claimed the kitchen was too small to do any serious baking, but maybe cookies weren't that serious in Millie's book. Truth be told, the thought of Millie not stopping by the guesthouse anymore to bake made me sad. She could be a handful, but I enjoyed her company. Plus, I needed her to keep bailing me out with breakfast dishes so the guests would have appetizing food to eat.

"Did you come from the town offices?" Millie's words dripped with faux innocence. I knew she had an ulterior motive.

Apparently Mike did too because his gaze narrowed and his hand hesitated as he pulled a chocolate-chip cookie out of the bag. "Yes, why?"

Millie played with the tablecloth avoiding Mike's eyes. "I was just wondering...you know, because you're right next to the police station there, if you've heard anything further about the skeleton they found earlier this morning?"

Mike tortured her by biting into the cookie and making a show of chewing slowly before answering. "Well, as a matter of fact I did."

"And...?" my mother and Millie both said, leaning in toward Mike with eager looks.

"Early assessment is that the skeleton was there for almost three hundred years. I guess it's pretty hard to date exactly, but the medical examiner used to be a forensic anthropologist so he knows old bones."

"Did they find any more clues inside the wall?" Millie asked.

Mike shook his head. "Nothing but a bunch of plaster. They did identify the ring and they're pretty sure the skeleton is Jedediah Biddeford based on the ring and an old fracture on his leg."

"Aha!" My mother straightened and pulled the head of her shovel out of the ground, showing the most animation I'd seen since I'd arrived. "That settles it then. If Jedediah Biddeford really did come back from Europe, then there's a good chance he brought the treasure back with him. And that treasure is buried somewhere on the property of the Oyster Cove Guesthouse."

Chapter Seven

Nero scanned the activity under the tent at the town common, his intelligent gaze coming to rest on Josie. She was talking to Myron Remington at the Oyster Cove Guesthouse display table. Nero felt sorry for Myron. He knew that many of the townspeople gossiped about him behind his back but then pandered to him in person because he was in control of the money. Try as he might, Nero would never understand the humans' obsession with money, nor how acquiring it could make them do unspeakable things.

"Hurry up, the gang's waiting." Marlowe had trotted ahead, her black-and-orange tail high in the air. They were heading toward the bait wharf at the town dock where they often met with their other feline friends.

The others would have heard about the discovery of the skeleton by now and would want all the juicy details. He hated to tell them that their excitement would be in vain; there was nothing left to decipher after all these years. Hopefully they wouldn't be too disappointed. Lying around all day in the sun could get boring and he was sure the others were as eager as he was to dig into a good investigation. Then again, judging by the behavior of the guests at the guesthouse, the cats might get that chance sooner than they thought.

Nero followed Marlowe past the colorful boats bobbing in the cove, down the long wharf and up the ramp to the bait dock. It was a mystery why the humans avoided this dock. He'd see them giving it a wide birth, covering their noses and making faces as they walked past.

The bait wharf had its own unique ambiance. The lapping of waves, the briny scent of ocean and rotting fish were pleasant, the incessant cawing of the gulls not so much. The gulls could be a nuisance, especially if they swooped down at you. Luckily there were plenty of old lobster traps to hide behind if that happened. Still, Nero knew to be careful where he stepped. One panicked misstep could land you in the cold Atlantic.

"Heard someone got iced up at the guesthouse again," said Stubbs, an orange-striped tabby with a stub of a tail who was batting at a rope dangling from the side of a lobster trap. Stubbs had a habit of talking in old-time detective speak, which Nero presumed was a result of his human reading too many Raymond Chandler books to him.

"Not exactly," Marlowe said. "Well, I guess he got iced at some point but not in our time."

"How long do you think he was in there?" Juliette curled her fluffy gray tail around her as she settled on top of one of the lobster pots.

"Probably about two hundred and fifty years." Boots licked his paw, the white boot contrasting with the black on the rest of his leg, then smoothed one of his long whiskers.

"How do you know that?" Harry, a fluffy Maine coon, asked.

Boots gave him a look of superiority. Boots could be that way. He fancied himself cleverer than the others, which could be annoying at times. But he had a good heart and mad detective skills, so Nero let it pass. "I used my superior sense to find out who the victim was and did the math."

"You mean you overheard Sheriff Chamberlain." Poe, a gray mix, leveled Boots with a green-eyed stare.

"Well, am I correct?" Boots ignored Poe and turned to Nero.

"Indeed. The body has been there for exactly two hundred and fifty years." Nero used the word "exactly" loosely. His superior senses enabled him to deduct an average or expected amount of time, but he couldn't be sure. Then again, none of the other cats could either, so he might as well try to sound smart while he could.

A shadow loomed from above and the cats all ducked. A seagull!

Splat! A white-and-orange dropping landed on the ground in the middle of the cats who had formed a conversational circle. The gull's raucous laughter echoed as it swooped up into the sky.

"Darn things are getting aggressive again." Juliette checked her fluffy tail for bird droppings.

"Maybe it wasn't so bad when they were dying off." Stubbs eyed the splatter as they all shifted over to a non-soiled part of the wharf.

"If the crime is that old it doesn't sound like anything we could dig our claws into," Harry said, once they were settled. "Murder most likely. I mean, how else would a skeleton get inside a wall? My informant down at the police station, Louie Two Paws, has told me the victim was all bones, and not even delicious ones either. Not that we would eat human bones. And the police think it was Jedediah Biddeford, the guy who built your very own Oyster Cove Guesthouse."

"Indeed." Again Nero acted like he already knew all this, but in fact he'd only suspected. He'd have found out from Millie or Josie eventually, but it was good to have confirmation straight from the police source.

"But how can we investigate?" Boots preened his long whiskers, curling them up at the end. "There are no clues left to stimulate our superior brain power or suspects alive to spy on."

Another shadow loomed and the cats ducked again.

"Darn gulls." Marlowe looked up at the sky.

"They seem healthy now," Nero said. Earlier that summer the gull population had been mysteriously dying off. That was resolved now and, while Nero was glad the creatures were not dying, he still wished they would stop tormenting the cats.

"From my bird's-eye view from the belfry, it seems as if there are more and more of them swooping around the cliffs every day. I don't know if that's a good thing or not. I wouldn't mind if they left us alone." Juliette lived at the rectory and had full range of the entire place, including the belfry. She'd invited Nero up there once and the view was astounding. No wonder she spent so much time up there.

All the other cats nodded. The gulls took pleasure in

tormenting the cats. Nero had tried to catch one once, and it was not an easy endeavor. Besides, it could be very dangerous as their beaks were sharp.

"Too bad your bird's-eye view couldn't show us who killed Jedediah Biddeford," Poe said. "Then we'd be able to solve a case even the police probably can't."

Juliette sighed, the white star on her forehead scrunching together. "No, it can't, but it can show me that the town has gone crazy for shovels."

"Yeah, at first I hoped maybe they were all trying to bury bodies. But then I realized there was no way all those people bumped someone off," Stubbs said. "Turns out it's because of the treasure curse."

"You mean the humans believe in that?" Boots looked incredulous. "I would think they'd be smarter."

"When it comes to treasure, you never can tell what people will do. They go crazy," Stubbs said.

Juliette nodded. "Sometimes even so far as to commit murder."

"I wouldn't put it past the Biddefords to try to bump off the competition," Marlowe said. "We heard two of them arguing about a secret book earlier."

"You don't say." Poe turned his gaze to Marlowe. "Tell me more."

Marlowe shuffled uneasily. "Well, we're not sure what kind of book. But it sounded important."

"A treasure map?" Stubbs asked.

Marlowe scrunched up her nose. "I don't think so."

"Well, what did your human, Josie, make of the argument?" Harry asked.

"She didn't hear it," Marlowe said.

"So she knows nothing of this supposed secret book?" Poe asked.

Marlowe washed behind her ears. "No. Hopefully it won't become important if someone is bumped off because I have no idea how we would let her in on it."

"We'd have to look for evidence in their rooms, I suppose," Nero said. Then he added, "But let's not get too eager for nefarious activity."

"Right," Stubbs said. "We have a skeleton mystery to look into."

"But maybe that's how Jedediah ended up inside the wall. Someone killed him over money," Poe suggested.

"If that's true that means the treasure is long gone." Nero hopped up onto one of the lobster crates, looking up anxiously to make sure another gull was not about to launch a sneak attack.

"Judging by the number of people I saw running around with shovels, the humans don't think the treasure is long gone," Juliette said.

"Sometimes they lack common sense," Boots said.

"Your spot on the belfry sure is good for getting an overview of what is going on in town," Stubbs said. "Easy to get the dime on someone that way."

"My home at the rectory is good for more than that. I get to hear and see all sorts of things. Like the odd confession I overheard when I was napping in the confessional box this morning."

"You nap in the confessional box?" Poe asked. "That sounds sacrilegious."

Juliette's fur ruffled in offense. "Well, I don't do it to overhear confessions unless we are investigating a murder where confessions might come in handy. But it's a lovely place to nap. All dark and cozy and silent. It's rarely used. I didn't realize Father Timothy would be hearing a confession and I was fast asleep. By the time I realized what was going on, it was too late to leave."

Nero's whiskers twitched. He moved closer to Juliette. "What did you hear?"

Juliette's eyes took on a faraway look as her mind worked to conjure up the conversation. "It was a woman, and she was confessing how regretful it was that she was forced to betray those close to her."

Chapter Eight

I let myself in through the back door in the kitchen of the guesthouse shortly before supper, loaded with bags of ingredients for the peanut-butter-banana bread I was planning to make that night. Millie had said that loaf cakes were the easiest thing to bake, so I was going to trust her on that. I needed something easy. And even though my first few attempts at baking had turned out as hard as hockey pucks, I was still hopeful.

I'd barely gotten the ingredients on the counter when I heard a ruckus in the parlor. The Biddefords were at it again. I figured now would be a good time to talk to them about digging up the yard. I headed toward the parlor, passing a pile of shovels in the foyer on the way. Flora was going to have a fit. Shovels brought in dirt and she barely vacuumed as it was.

"It's not my fault the *Shmithsh* canceled the order for twenty miniature *cheesh cashtles*," Paula slurred.

"Well, it certainly isn't mine," Carla said.

"Children!" Doris yelled. "It's not anybody's fault. Things happen in business. All this infighting is making things worse."

"You can say that again," Earl said.

Just as I suspected, the entire family was dressed for

digging—old jeans, T-shirts. Earl and Arlene's were of the designer variety, of course. Doris even had mud on her feet. I glanced out the window. Had she already started digging?

"Ahem." They hadn't noticed me lurking in the doorway, so I cleared my throat to capture their attention. "I'd appreciate it if you didn't bring dirty shovels into the house. In fact, I'd appreciate it if you didn't dig up the yard, either."

Doris hurried over to me. "Don't you worry, dear. We'll fill the holes back in. We're just looking for the treasure buried by our ancestor." Doris glanced behind her for confirmation and the others nodded.

"Yeah. We won't disrupt your property or anything," Bob said.

I gazed at them skeptically then back at the shovels. Earl saw me looking and hastily added, "We'll keep the shovels in that old carriage house so the guesthouse doesn't get dirty."

He pointed toward the dilapidated building that had been a carriage house when the mansion was in service. Even though it was overgrown with vines and needed a paint job badly, Mike had assured me it was still safe when I'd bought the place. At least if they kept their shovels there that would keep most of the dirt out.

But there was something else bothering me. It was the way Doris had said *our ancestor* in reference to the treasure. It made me wonder, if there really was any treasure, then who actually owned it? Wouldn't it belong to me since I now owned the property?

I didn't think now was a good time to bring that up;

I could practically see dollar signs in the Biddefords' eyes. Odds were against a treasure being buried out there anyway and even more odds against them finding it. I'd cross that bridge when and *if* we came to it.

Earl went to the foyer and started gathering up the shovels and I returned to the kitchen. I laid out the ingredients on the counter. Peanut butter, bananas, flour, milk, sugar, baking soda and baking powder.

I pulled the old jadcite green batter bowls from the cupboard, preheated the oven and started mixing things together. Millie would've been proud. Of course, when she baked, she didn't spew flour in a ten-foot radius all around her like I did. Guess I still had plenty of room for improvement.

I kept one eye on the ingredients and the other on the yard. A movement coming from the front of the house caught my eye. It was Bob. He rushed past the window, a shovel clutched in his hand. Getting an early jump on his siblings?

He headed toward the carriage house, glancing behind him as if to make sure no one had followed.

Did Bob know something about the treasure that the others didn't? How would they go about locating Jed's cache, I wondered? How would they know where to dig? Were they just going to randomly dig holes? Or did they have a plan in mind?

I ladled the batter into two loaf pans. It *looked* good. I bent down and sniffed. And it *smelled* good. The real test would be if it *tasted* good. Only one way to find out. I opened the oven and shoved them inside.

No sooner had I finished that when a loud knock

on the front door echoed through the house. I brushed the flour off my hands and rushed to the front. I had no idea who it could be since the door was unlocked during the day and the guests just walked in. Maybe it was a tourist wanting to check out the place to rent a room at a later date.

I'm sure I didn't hide my disappointment very well when I opened the door to reveal that it was Sheriff Chamberlain. Nevertheless, I invited him into the foyer.

"Hey, Josie, I just wanted to come and retrieve the police tape and markers from the crime scene."

"You're done with your investigation?" I asked as I led him toward the west wing.

"Yep, done as we're gonna be." Seth spread his hands. "I mean, what's to investigate?"

I unlocked the door and we proceeded over to the area where the skeleton had been found. Sheriff Chamberlain pulled the crime-scene tape off the edges of the wall and picked up the yellow crime-scene markers.

"So you're not going to go figure out who killed him?" I asked. I know the guy was killed a long time ago, but it didn't seem right not to bring his killer to justice, even if we couldn't arrest them and bring them to trial.

Seth leveled a look at me. "Josie. There would be no suspects to interrogate. We're not even sure who the victim was, though it probably was Jedediah. We researched his whereabouts. We know he went to Europe and supposedly never came back but his death was never recorded over there either."

"Did they record deaths back then?"

What if Jed had fallen into the sea on the way back or something? Surely someone had written something down? But if it wasn't Jed in the wall, then who was it?

Seth shrugged. "They did record deaths back then, but if he died alone somewhere and they didn't know who he was, his name wouldn't be on any death certificates, so..." Seth shrugged and let his voice trail off.

"I guess you have a point. There's not much to go on after all this time, but you'd think his relatives would want closure."

"So far not one of them have come to me for it," Seth said. "I mean, it's not like any of them actually knew the guy and I don't want to take up valuable police resources on an investigation that no one cares about."

What else did the police have to do? There wasn't much crime in Oyster Cove. But given the way the Biddefords were acting about the treasure and the fact that the whole town had bought shovels, a police presence might be needed in my very own backyard in the not-too-distant future.

I glanced out the window, my brow furrowing as I saw a form in the shrubbery. A form with a shovel. Thankfully it wasn't dead. Paula lay curled up under the azalea bush like an innocent child—if innocent children passed out from drinking and hugged shovels in their sleep. As I watched, her nose twitched—that's how I knew she was alive.

"Yeah, I guess they're pretty far removed. So that's it then? Case closed?" I asked.

Seth put the last of the police equipment into a bag

and turned to the door. "Yep. The room is officially cleared and you can start working in here again."

Good thing I'd given Ed the rest of the day off. He'd resisted going home, puttering around the grounds instead, but I knew he hadn't started in the conservatory yet. This way I could just have him continue in the ballroom. I'd told him he needn't stay but I kept seeing him around and whenever I asked him why he hadn't left he simply said he was tending to "this and that." I guess he felt guilty about going home since I'd given him the day off with pay. Call me an old softy but I knew he was supplementing his Social Security income and I didn't want him to miss a day's pay just because someone had shoved a body inside my wall three centuries ago.

My phone chirped, and I pulled it out of my pocket. A bright spot in the day! It was my daughter, Emma. I couldn't help but smile. Emma lived halfway across the country and I didn't get to see her often, so her phone calls were like balm for my soul. I loved hearing stories about her job. She'd recently started working at the FBI, so I figured she would get a kick out of the skeleton story.

"Gram told me you found another dead body," Emma said as soon as I answered the phone.

Leave it to my mother to spread distorted news as fast as she could. Emma and my mom were close, and that was a good thing, except sometimes they were a little too close. I didn't mind so much except my mother tended to be overly dramatic and sometimes she exaggerated when she passed on information to Emma.

"Well, it wasn't exactly a body, at least it hasn't been for quite some time." I didn't want Emma to worry. Or think that I was some kind of weird murderer attractor.

"Gram was a little vague." The tone of concern in Emma's voice squeezed my heart. It was sweet that she was worried, but it was my job to worry about her, not the other way around. That would come much later in life if I turned out like my mother, I hasten to add. "Turns out there was a skeleton buried in the wall here. Sheriff Chamberlain says he's been dead almost three hundred years."

"No kidding. Gram said something about treasure, too." Emma's concern turned to excitement. That's good, it meant she wouldn't be worried about me.

"Apparently there was some curse about the treasure and now the whole town is going crazy thinking they are going to find it in the yard here."

"Oh, that sounds messy. What about the investigation?" Emma asked. She'd always been interested in investigations, so it was no surprise when she'd gone to college to study criminology and then jumped at the FBI's job offer upon graduation. Who knew her mother would end up with a dead body and an old skeleton in her guesthouse? Maybe the abundance of homicides would make her want to move to town. We could use her help if dead bodies continued to crop up.

"There won't be one. Sheriff Chamberlain pointed out that there are no suspects still alive and no one to arrest. They aren't even a hundred-percent sure who the victim is."

"Hmm...still seems like one should get to the

bottom of what happened. Maybe he should send it to a forensic anthropologist or something and have them look into it. I could hook him up, but there's probably a backlog."

"I could mention it to him. No one here seems interested in it, though. Not even the dead guy's family."

"Oh, right. They're staying at the guesthouse. Were they upset?"

"Hardly. More like excited once they concluded the discovery of the skeleton meant his treasure could still be buried outside." I peered out the window to see if any digging had started. Thankfully not yet. Paula was still asleep in the shrub.

"So things are going good otherwise?"

"Fabulous."

"And Uncle Tommy's friend, Mike? How are things going with him?" Emma's voice held a hint of mischief and hopefulness.

That must have been my mother exaggerating again. "He hasn't written me up for any building code violations yet."

"Gram implied he might be inspecting more than just the guesthouse..."

"Gram implies a lot of things that are not correct. There's nothing going on." I put that to rest as soon as possible. The last thing I needed was my daughter digging into my love life. Or lack thereof.

"Well, if there was, I think that would be great. I mean, I love Dad and everything, but you deserve to be happy."

"Thanks, honey, I'm glad you feel that way." At

least if I ever did start dating, Emma wouldn't be one
of those adult children who protested their mother ever
being with anyone but their father. It made me wonder
how she felt about Clive's many lady friends. A pang of
jealousy surfaced. Did Emma like them? Then again,
how could she get to know any of them? His bedroom
had a revolving door. I assumed Clive still liked to
have several on reserve just like he had when we were
married.

I started toward the foyer. The Biddefords had
agreed to keep the shovels in the carriage house, but I
wanted to make sure the entranceway stayed clear and
clean. I didn't want any prospective guests thinking I
ran a dirty show here. The shovels were all gone, but
clumps of dirt remained. I'd have to clean those up,
Lord knew Flora wouldn't do it.

"So how are things with you?" I asked to move the
conversation away from me and Mike.

"Fabulous..." Emma proceeded to tell me about
what was going on in her life while I got the broom
and dustpan out of the pantry. I was glad that she was
settling in to her adult life. She was healthy, had friends
and a good social life and was happy at work. It was all
a mother could ask. Now, if I could just get *my* mother
to stop worrying her about dead bodies and getting her
hopes up about romantic prospects, things would be
great.

*

As I cleaned up the mess, I mused about how quickly
Flora had trained me to do pretty much everything on

my own. Honestly, I had wondered more than once if I should keep her on. But she was a great-grandmother on Social Security. She needed the money. Besides, Millie had said that Flora had provided decades of loyal service to the guesthouse and that counted for something. And she did do *some* of the cleaning. Besides, the dirt was easy to clean up, just a few swoops into the dustpan and it was gone.

I heard a door open upstairs and glanced through the railing to the hallway out of habit. The front foyer was large and had a grand staircase that opened to a gallery hallway that looked down on the foyer. I saw Flora's orthopedic shoes coming out of the middle room.

Surprise, surprise, she'd actually been cleaning the rooms!

Not wanting to disturb Flora if she was in a room-cleaning mood, I started back toward the pantry with my dustpan full of dirt.

"Oh, there you are."

I spun around to see that Arlene had snuck up on me. She had a sour look on her face. I half expected to see a shovel clutched in her hands but they were empty. The smell of Chanel No. 5 wafted around her so strongly it almost gave me an asthma attack.

"Can I help you?" I asked, stepping back out of range of her perfume.

She made a face. "Well, I certainly hope so. The accommodations...our room...it's deplorable!"

"How so?" I thought the rooms at the Oyster Cove Guesthouse were quite nice. They were loaded with antiques, decorated in lovely colors with wallpaper and rugs suitable to the time period and had been all redone less than five years prior.

"Our room hasn't been cleaned. We'd appreciate it if you could send up the maid. I don't believe she's been in there since we arrived." Arlene made a big production out of sneezing. "I'm allergic to dirt and soot, you know."

Maybe she should back off on the perfume dousing. I was willing to bet that was what was making her sneeze. But I knew better than to argue with the guests. The customer was always right. Besides, I'd just seen Flora come out of her room so I was sure it would be at least a little bit cleaner when she went back.

"I'll have it cleaned right away." Sometimes it was beneficial to let guests think they'd bossed you around.

She huffed and turned to leave, practically bowling over Doris.

"What are you doing?" Doris looked at her suspiciously. "Are you pumping Josie for information on likely places where the treasure might be buried?"

Arlene looked her mother-in-law up and down. No love lost there, I sensed. "Hardly. I'm just trying to get our room cleaned. I doubt there even is any treasure."

"Ha! Then you don't need to dig for it." Doris watched Arlene walk away then turned to me. "Say, you wouldn't have happened to find anything like an old map or any indication in the house of where the treasure could be?"

"No." Hadn't Millie mentioned an old book about the history of the Oyster Cove Guesthouse that she wanted for the table at the town celebration? Might that have some clue? Not that I believed in the treasure, but it might be worthwhile to browse through it. Of course, I wasn't going to mention that to Doris.

"Dang. Well, if you think of anything speak up."

"Oh, I will."

Movement outside caught my eye and I glanced out the narrow window beside the door where Bob was rushing by with a shovel.

"Those darn nincompoops. I told him to wait until dark," Doris said.

"Dark? Then how would you see what you're digging?" I asked.

"Headlamps."

"Speaking of digging, I want to make sure there're not a lot of holes in the ground. I don't want a liability issue."

"Oh, no, don't worry. We're gonna fill them in just like we said. And we'll put the shovels in the carriage house and wipe our feet so we don't track dirt in."

"I hope you will." I showed her the dirt in the dustpan. "You've already tracked quite a bit in. And I still think it might be smarter to dig in daylight."

Doris shook her head. "Nah. If they did that, then each one would see where the other one was digging."

"You mean they'd steal the treasure from each other?"

Doris sighed. "Sadly, I think they would. I mean, they are my children and I love them, but they have their faults."

"All kids do."

"I made them make a pact that we'd share the treasure but I'm not so sure they'll stick to it. They haven't played nice together since they were toddlers. Take the cheese-sculpture business, for example. My husband Barney and I built that up from nothing. We started off whittling Wisconsin cheddar and ended with sculpting masterpieces of Gruyère."

I nodded with empathy even though I wanted to get back to the kitchen and throw away the dustpan full of dirt I was holding.

"Once Barney was gone, the kids took over. Big mistake. Turns out that when you inherit a business you don't take as much care as when you build it up. You don't work as hard. I'm afraid things are going downhill." Doris flopped into a chair and I suddenly felt sorry for her.

As if proving her point, Bob's voice wafted down from above. He was arguing with someone, but we couldn't make out exactly what he was saying or who he was arguing with.

"See what I mean?" Doris pointed up.

"Well, siblings always fight and hopefully things will pick up with the business," I assured her, for lack of anything better to say.

"If we found the treasure it sure would. 'Course, I doubt any of my kids would actually use the money for the business." Her eyes turned steely. "But I would. In fact, I'd do just about anything to get some extra cash flow to save it. Barney would have wanted that."

If the treasure actually belongs to you, I thought. Again, I didn't see the point of voicing that opinion. No sense in pissing off paying guests over something that was unlikely to happen.

She sighed and pushed up from the chair. "Anyway, I don't know how those kids turned out all wrong. I tried my best." Doris made a face, her eyes crinkling and her nose twitching as she sniffed. "What's that smell? Is something burning in the kitchen?"

Chapter Nine

I rushed back to the kitchen to see smoke billowing from the oven. Luckily I had the presence of mind to grab some oven mitts before ripping open the door. I used the mitts to fan the smoke away from my face as I bent down to inspect my loaf cakes that now resembled shrunken dried-out old leather. I pulled them out and slapped both on the counter, then waved frantically and prayed the sprinkler system the previous town building inspector had made me put in didn't go off and soak everything.

I rushed over to open the back door to let out some of the smoke. It was getting dark and I could barely make out the moonlit ocean and the silhouette of the Smugglers Bay Inn beyond the tiny little lights that danced over my yard like fireflies. Except they weren't fireflies. They were little flashlights in the hands of the people digging up the yard.

And it was a lot more than just the Biddefords.

I squinted into the night. Who was out there? My mom, for one. I saw her by the old oak tree jabbing her shovel into the earth. Leave it to Mom, that was probably a good spot for buried treasure. Didn't pirates always bury their treasure under a tree?

Doris Biddeford was now out there too, digging

in the mound of the hill we thought was an old bottle
dump. Another good location.

But the number of flashlights indicated there were
a lot more than just my mom and the Biddefords digging. Just how many people were out there?

I stepped on to the stairs and a shadowy figure ran
by my feet. Nero. He darted over to the old rose arbor
and started digging. Apparently even the cats wanted in
on the treasure hunt.

Darn! Was that a light bobbing over from the Smugglers Bay Inn? Even Stella was getting in on this crazy
treasure hunt. And was that figure around the edge of
the property Myron Remington? The town's richest
banker wanted a chance at buried treasure, too.

What was wrong with people? More interested in
treasure than finding out who had killed Jedediah Biddeford or how he ended up in the wall? And how *had* he
ended up in there? Had he really brought treasure back
and then someone killed him for it? And if so, wouldn't
that person have taken the treasure? All these people
were on a fool's errand. No treasure existed in my yard,
I was sure of it. But maybe I should go out and dig,
too...just in case.

I considered it for a second until a whiff of
burned peanut-butter-banana bread reminded me that
I had more important things to do. I needed to mix
up another batch of batter and get it in the oven
and figure out what to cook for breakfast the next
morning. I didn't have time to go on any treasure
hunts.

*

Nero stopped sharpening his claws on the soft rotted wood of the old rose arbor and sniffed the air. "What is that noxious odor?"

"Smells like burned bananas." Marlowe's eyes flicked to the kitchen window. "Josie must be baking again."

Nero sighed. "I do hope she can master that. Millie is right, the guests do want good food."

"But if she doesn't, maybe Millie will come over more often and help her?"

"That would be good, but Millie needs to have her fun too. Can't expect her to bake for the guests every day. Josie needs to learn."

"I suppose." Marlowe's eyes reflected gold in the light of the moon as she watched the people walking around the yard with their shovels and flashlights. "Silly humans. I could have told them nothing is buried here. I know. I sniffed the entire estate."

"Me too." Nero watched the other cat closely. "But did you discover anything interesting while you were sniffing?"

Marlowe jerked her head back to look at Nero. "Interesting? No. There is no treasure, I assure you."

Nero washed behind his left ear. See? The other cat still had a lot to learn. "Not treasure, true..."

"What, then?"

"Nefarious intent and betrayal. I smelled it on the searchers. Someone is thinking dark thoughts."

Marlowe looked back at the searchers. "Do you think that has anything to do with the confession Juliette overheard?"

"Perhaps."

"And do you think it has something to do with the guests here?"

"Likely. They do have issues. The mother made them swear that they would split the treasure, but I think some of them want to take it for themselves."

"I think all of them want to. But since there is no treasure, there will be no problem there."

"No." Nero stopped washing and watched the lights bobbing in the yard. He was going to have a heck of a job early tomorrow morning checking the grounds and filling in any holes the diggers had forgotten to fill. He didn't want to leave any open for someone to trip into. That might reflect badly on the guesthouse. "I think we need to watch them carefully, though. There is dissension in the ranks."

"I'll say," Marlowe agreed. "Weird bunch. Not even interested in the old bones of their ancestor. I must say, I'm a bit disappointed that the police have dropped the case."

"Me too. But you know we sniffed that wall for hours and not one clue. Not one old scent. Nothing."

"I know." Marlowe's voice dripped with disappointment.

Nero glanced back to see Josie's silhouette moving around in the kitchen window. Hopefully she was mixing up something that would be suitable for the town celebration. "Looks like Josie has her hands full in the kitchen. We'll need to watch these diggers carefully. It's up to us to make sure the guests don't leave the yard in a shambles . . . or do something even worse."

Chapter Ten

I slept like a log. You'd think I would have tossed and turned, what with the discovery of a skeleton in my wall and half the town digging up my yard, but stress always made me sleepy. I'd fallen asleep with the cats snuggled against me in the bed around midnight only to jerk awake one minute before my alarm went off at seven. I rushed downstairs to get breakfast ready. Luckily, I'd picked out something that I could whip together quickly.

I got bacon and sausages going on the stove. Those were the mainstays of a good breakfast as far as I was concerned. And, of course, given the Biddefords' love of pancakes, I whipped up some batter. I might have put in too much sugar—I mean the one tablespoon in the recipe hardly seemed like enough—but hopefully they wouldn't notice. I quickly diced up some fruit and put it in Millie's great-grandma's cut-glass boat-shaped fruit bowl. That always made a great presentation.

Now for omelets. I set some butter heating in a few pans, then beat together some eggs, water, salt and pepper. Was I supposed to be paying attention to the ratio? The mixture looked okay, so I poured it into the pans. Now what? I tilted the pans so the egg mixture coated the bottom and waited until it looked like it was cooking and tossed in some ham and cheese I'd chopped the night before. Hmm...it looked like it needed something else. I rummaged in the fridge and pulled out some spinach. A little greenery always adds a nice touch. I threw it in at the last minute. Hmmm... shouldn't it get wilty? I didn't have time to wait for that.

For once I had timed things perfectly and it was ready by the time I heard the Biddefords stirring upstairs.

I rushed it into the dining room where coffee was already percolating in the old-fashioned urn. Say what you will about Flora but at least she always put on the coffee. That was probably because she wanted some herself, but I wasn't about to complain.

The Biddefords shuffled in and filled their mugs. Good thing I'd remembered to put out Carla's Yale mug. She looked like she was in a bad mood and I didn't want to suffer her wrath. In fact, they all looked a little worse for wear. No doubt they'd been up late digging.

I glanced outside at the yard but true to their word they'd filled in the holes, though the grass looked a little ratty. I had to admit my landscaping hadn't been that great to begin with. Apparently no one had dug up treasure because they weren't celebrating.

"No treasure last night?" I asked as they filled their plates and took their seats at the long table.

"Not for lack of trying, though." Doris shoved a forkful of pancakes into her mouth and chewed. Then she glanced around the table suspiciously at her children. "I mean, one of you didn't find it, did you?"

Paula hiccupped and shook her head, looking at her mother with big, innocent eyes over her coffee mug.

Her face was still scratched from the shrub she'd fallen asleep in the day before.

"Well, I certainly didn't," Carla said. "But maybe someone else did?" She glanced across the table at Bob's empty seat.

Doris followed her gaze. "Where is Bob? Has anyone seen him?"

Earl shrugged. "I didn't hear him moving around in his room. Maybe he's sleeping in. Knowing Bob, he was the last one up digging. He always did try to one-up the rest of us."

Carla's eyes narrowed. "You don't think he found the treasure and took off with it, do you?"

"Where would he go and how would he get there? We only have three rental cars between us and they are all in the driveway." Earl looked at me. "Bob didn't leave in a taxi or anything early this morning, did he?"

I shook my head.

"I'm just glad we don't have to share the pancakes," Henry said as he raised a forkful of golden pancakes dripping with syrup.

I smiled pleasantly. At least no one had said the pancakes were too sweet. In fact, they seemed to be enjoying them. Maybe I was on to something with the extra sugar.

Mereeoow.

The sound came from outside, and it wasn't the cat's normal meow. It sounded panicked. My heart jerked. Had an animal gotten them? I rushed over to the window, shoving aside the sheer blind that was fluttering in the breeze and looked out.

I didn't see any cats. Nor did I hear any more pan-icked meowing. I scanned the yard, then the field, but the only movement was a lobster boat motoring around in the cove picking up traps and a few seagulls circling above it.

I turned back to the room in time to see Paula spit out some omelet. Gross.

"What's the matter with you?" Doris asked.

Paula made a face. "The spinach in there is weird."

Arlene nodded and pinched up a spinach leaf between her thumb and forefinger and held it up. "They're sup-posed to be wilted. This isn't cooked." She leveled a look at me.

Who knew you were supposed to put them in sooner so they cooked all the way?

"It's a new thing. More healthy this way. A lot of the vitamins are lost when you cook it." I had no idea if it was true, but I thought I'd recovered quite nicely.

"I heard that the sheriff came by yesterday," Doris said.

"Yes, he cleared the crime scene."

"Did he say what happened?"

"Not much more than what we learned yesterday, but he did think it was Jedediah Biddeford."

"Huh, go figure. I knew it was him." Doris looked around the table. "Should we have a funeral?"

The kids shook their heads.

"Who would pay for that?" Arlene asked.

"Good point," Doris said. "Maybe we could make a cheese sculpture in his honor. I mean, it's not like we knew him. No sense in spending money on a funeral when there are no friends or family to attend."

"Maybe just have him buried in the old family cemetery." Paula had a Baileys Irish Cream nip in her hand and was pouring it on the pancakes.

"Well, that would be up to Josie. She owns it now." Doris raised a brow in my direction.

The old Biddeford family cemetery was at the west edge of the property. I'd seen the moss-covered slabs ringed with a black wrought-iron fence once when Millie had taken me back to show me some of the acreage. It was overgrown and barely accessible and I was sure no one had been buried there in two hundred years.

"I guess it's okay. I don't think they actually bury people in old family plots like that anymore, do they?"

Doris shrugged and then she laughed. "Maybe we can do it ourselves. We have shovels."

"Speaking of which, we put the shovels away in the carriage house like you wanted, Josie," Earl said.

"Thank you."

A movement outside caught my eye. It was Mike Sullivan. I'd forgotten he was coming to inspect an old toolshed that I'd had Ed replace the roof on. I was looking into hiring someone to work on the landscaping and they'd need a place to store the tools. I watched as he headed down the path.

Merow!

This time it sounded like the same high-pitched caterwauling that had happened when they'd found the skeleton. If I wasn't mistaken, the noise was coming from the direction in which Mike was heading. Mike was good with cats; if something was wrong he would help them.

"I hate to be a complainer," Arlene said, inspecting her fingernails for dirt—not that dirt would dare stick to her, "but I would appreciate it if we could get some maid service in our room. It's still dirty like I told you yesterday."

I bit back a sarcastic remark. Arlene was the type that was never happy. I'd seen Flora in there cleaning, so I knew it had been cleaned. Then again, Flora wasn't the best cleaner so maybe I should go in myself and make sure it was spotless.

Merooo!

This time it was loud. Everyone looked toward the window.

"What is that?" Paula asked. "Is that those cats?"

"Yes, they meow like that sometimes."

Doris's eyes narrowed. "The last time they did that we found a skeleton in the wall."

I forced a laughed. "What are the chances of that happening again?"

Doris craned to look out the window as another panicked meow drifted in. "I don't know, but something urgent must be going on out there. Look." She pointed and I tilted my head so I could see what she was pointing at.

It was Mike Sullivan and he was running toward the house.

My heart jerked. Was one of the cats in trouble? Maybe one was hurt badly and he was running to call for help.

As I ran into the hallway, I heard the kitchen door whip open and Mike's footsteps as he rushed toward the dining room.

"What is it? Are the cats okay?" The tightness in my chest made me realize how fond I'd grown of the cats. I hated the thought of one of them being hurt. Not to mention Millie would kill me if anything happened to them.

"Where's the fire?" Doris had come out into the hall and was standing behind me. Wait, was she making a reference to my loaf cakes that kept burning?

"There's no fire," Mike panted. "My phone battery is dead and we need to call Seth Chamberlain. There's a body down by the pond and it doesn't look good."

*

"Well, at least Mike will get the ball rolling. If we waited for Josie to understand what our different cries mean this one might turn into a skeleton too." Nero eyed the body floating facedown at the edge of the pond. Unfortunately, this body wasn't almost three hundred years old. And even more unfortunately, it was the body of one of the guests.

"It doesn't bode well that another one of the guests has died here." Marlowe's voice held a tinge of guilt.

Nero understood why the other cat felt guilty. He felt that way himself. They'd been asleep (literally) on the job a few weeks ago and a guest had been killed inside the B&B. The Oyster Cove Guesthouse was their responsibility now and being unaware that someone was being murdered, and thus not taking steps to prevent it, had weighed heavily on him. Luckily it didn't seem like it had hurt business, but the results could have been disastrous.

And now there'd been another murder and they hadn't prevented that one either. Hopefully this wouldn't stain the guesthouse's reputation.

"What's going on? I could hear you guys all the way over at the Smugglers Bay Inn where I was under the deck looking for handouts." Poe pushed his way through the shrubs.

"Yeah, and you interrupted my nap in the morning sun." Juliette ducked under a pine bough, her eyes growing wide when she saw the body.

"Oh . . . You've got a floater." Stubbs appeared from a small path that led up to the cliffs.

"Yeah, guess we messed up again," Marlowe said.

"Is it one of the guests?" Boots trotted to the edge of the pond and proceeded to inspect the body.

Nero sighed. "I'm afraid so."

"Hey, don't feel bad." Harry picked a burr from his fur. "It's not like you can watch over every piece of the property."

"Yeah, and this place was crawling with people last night," Juliette said.

"Tell me about it." Nero watched as Boots trotted gingerly around the body, taking care not to disturb anything. He'd already done his own inspection, but valued the others' opinions, even if Boots could act a bit uppity at times. "Were you guys here last night? Did you see any odd behavior from the humans?"

"Sorry, I was at the rectory all night," Juliette said.

"I wasn't here either, but people were acting weird all over town," Harry said. "Treasure fever."

"You think it was a townie who did it?" Poe asked.

Boots had finished with the body and come back to the others now standing at the edge of the clearing. They knew the humans would be there soon and wanted to blend into the background. It wouldn't do to have the humans suspect they were actually investigating.

"That's doubtful," Boots said. "Who would have motive? Makes more sense that one of the other guests did it since they know each other."

"Of course." Nero regretted the huffy tone in his voice, but it did get tedious when Boots stated the obvious as if he was the only one who would think of it. The other cat raised a brow at him, preening his long whiskers.

"I've had a gut feeling that something was going on with the guests," Nero said.

"This is good news," Harry said.

"Not so much for the body," Poe replied.

"Oh, sorry, yeah. What I meant was this is a fresh case. One we can really sink our claws into."

"First we start with the family members," Juliette said.

Marlowe nodded. "They smell sneaky."

"And a bit like Swiss cheese," Nero said. "They've been arguing a lot too. Especially with the victim."

"We should check out their things. One of them might have evidence," Harry said.

"Do you think they have any of those cheese sculptures in their rooms?" Stubbs's pink tongue darted out and licked his lips.

"No, I checked," Marlowe said. "Most I found was a few crumbs of Camembert."

"It might have something to do with that confession I overheard. It was a woman. And she mentioned something about betraying someone close to her," Juliette said.

"Not necessarily a family member, though," Boots pointed out. "One must use their superior feline brain cells to interpret the meaning of the clues."

Stubbs made a face. "Clues schmues. This guy was hit over the head with a shovel. They were digging for treasure. My bet is that he found something and someone wanted it. A fight ensued and the killer clonked him over the head and took the treasure for their own."

"Well, it wasn't this shovel." Boots gestured toward a shovel that lay next to the body. "There is no blood on the end."

"If the killer did steal the treasure, then someone is a little bit richer today. Maybe we should see who is spending more money," Poe said.

"Or hiding it in their rooms." Nero made a mental note to do a thorough inspection later.

The wail of a siren split the air and the cats shrunk back into the tall grass at the edge of the clearing. Now they could hear the pounding of footsteps and the shouts as the humans came running from the house.

"The humans are coming. Are you all sure you've checked the scene for clues? Once the humans come even the most subtle of clues will be obfuscated with weird smells and bumbling footsteps."

"I have what I need." Boots preened his whiskers.

"I'm good," Stubbs said.

"Ditto." Harry picked another burr out of his long fur.

"Me too," Juliette said.

"Good because the humans are going to need our help, especially Josie," Nero said. "We know about the confession and the argument about the secret book Marlowe and I overheard, but Josie doesn't have that advantage."

"Yeah," Marlowe added as the humans rushed out of the path practically falling all over each other. "And we better make it fast, before our dear Josie is accused of murder. Again."

Chapter Eleven

The pond was on the west edge of the property, too far to be visible from the house. Mike led us down a brambly path to the small muddy body of water. I supposed it had once been a lovely pond. Now, the rotted remnants of a wooden bench with a bush growing through it marred its appearance. The body, laying facedown at the water's edge with the shovel beside it, was a bit of a detractor as well. Even though he was facedown, I was certain that it was Bob Biddeford.

Nestled into the overgrowth on the other side of the pond were Nero and Marlowe. They weren't alone. Several other cats were crouched near them. A lovely fluffy Maine coon that looked like it needed brushing, the gray cat with white on its forehead that I recognized as Father Timothy's, an orange-striped one with a stubby tail, another gray cat, this one with shorter fur, and a black cat with white paws that had a know-it-all look on its face.

To my relief, Marlowe and Nero looked fine. Their alarming cries must have been to alert us to the body. This was the second time they'd done that. I guess I'd have to pay more attention to their meows in the future.

Doris's hands flew up to her face. "No! Is that Bobby?"

Paula went over to look at the body, her heel getting

stuck in the mud and causing her to stumble a bit. She crouched down, peering at the body but staying a distance away. She sucked in a breath then turned a sad face to her mother. "I'm afraid so."

I glanced over at Mike. I figured he wouldn't let anyone get too close. Rule No. 1 at a crime scene was don't mess with it.

Before Mike could say anything, though, Earl rushed over and grabbed onto Bob's ankle, trying to pull him out of the water even though we all knew it was too late.

Mike lunged for Earl and pulled him back. "Don't touch him. This is a crime scene. We need to leave it just like this for the police."

As if on cue, the sound of sirens split the air.

"Crime scene? Maybe he just fell in," Carla said. She'd gone over to console Doris and she, Doris and Paula stood in a circle, their arms around each other. Arlene stood off to the side appearing to be disinterested. Henry stood back, his arms over his chest, watching the family.

"Maybe it was the ghost," Doris said.

Earl jerked his head in her direction. "Ghost? You don't really think..." He swiveled his head back to look at Bob, his expression pensive as if he were considering the possibility that Jed's ghost had killed his brother. It was doubtful. I didn't know of any ghosts that could bash someone's head in, which is what had clearly happened to Bob.

"What do you suppose he was doing over here?" Carla asked.

"Looking for treasure like the rest of us, of course," Doris said.

Mike frowned down at the body. "Yeah, and I wonder if he found it and that's how he ended up in the pond."

"Maybe he just tripped and fell in by accident?" Henry said hopefully.

Mike glanced at me. Judging by the way the back of Bob's head was flattened, it didn't seem like he had fallen in by accident. And besides, who could drown in only a few inches of water without help? Unless he'd been getting into Paula's nips, he would've just picked himself up, brushed himself off and continued along the way.

I glanced at the cats. It was clear by the way Nero was looking at me that he didn't think it was an accident either.

The grass rustled behind us and we all turned to see my mother and Millie bursting out of the narrow path that led to the pond.

"See, what did I tell you, Josie's got another body!" Millie sounded almost excited. Then she looked around at the Biddefords, her face dropping. "Oh, I'm sorry. Is it one of the guests?"

Nero and Marlowe sprang into action upon seeing Millie and darted over to rub against her ankles. The other cats pulled back further into the overgrowth, satisfied that they'd seen all there was to see.

"It's Bob Biddeford," I said.

Millie eyed the Biddefords suspiciously and whispered, "Huh, really? Family dispute?"

"I have no idea," I whispered back.

"I heard they didn't get along very good," Mom said.

"Well, you were both here last night, did you see anything?"

Mom and Millie shook their heads. "We didn't think the treasure would be around here. We focused our efforts on the older side of the property."

More rustling from the path and Sheriff Seth Chamberlain and his deputies, Johnnie Sanders and Sheila Watts, came rushing into the clearing, cutting off any other queries I had with Mom and Millie.

"What happened?" Seth asked as they started getting out their crime-scene paraphernalia.

"Mike found him down by the pond," Millie said.

Seth turned to Mike. "What were you doing down here, Mike?"

Mike pointed toward the old toolshed, barely visible through the tall grass. "I came to inspect that. Josie had Ed do some repairs on it and it's on my inspection list."

Seth nodded, his eyes drifting back to the body. "Any ID on him?"

"It's my Bobby." Doris's voice cracked and she dissolved into tears.

Millie hustled over to her, put her arm around her and patted her shoulder soothingly. "Now, now, dear, it's going to be okay."

"My guess is it has something to do with this treasure, Sheriff," Johnnie said.

Seth nodded. "Good guess. Let's say this Bob character found the treasure and someone saw him, then clonked him over the head and took it from him." Seth glanced around at the ground as if looking for the hole the treasure might've come out of.

"Who would do that?" Carla asked.

I didn't say a word, but the way I looked over the Biddeford family might have given away my suspicions. Seth wasn't privy to their family dynamics, though. I'd have to let him find out for himself. But even though they argued a lot, killing your own brother—or son—was a whole different matter. Surely none of the Biddefords would stoop to murder?

"Just about anyone in town," Sheila shot over her shoulder from where she was crouched down in the muck beside the body taking pictures.

Seth nodded. "I heard a lot of people were out here last night. That true, Josie?"

"Well, I didn't see everyone who was out here, but there were a lot of flashlights," I said.

"Really?" Seth raised a brow at me. "And where were you?"

"I was inside preparing the breakfast for this morning," I said.

"And what about all your guests?"

"They were outside digging for treasure," I said. "Along with the rest of the town."

"It was dark, Sheriff, and hard to see who was who," Johnnie said. "There were people all over the place."

"Is that so? How would you know that, Johnnie?"

Johnnie's expression turned sheepish. "Well, I might've come here. The wife dragged me along."

Seth pressed his lips together. "Kinda odd. Two

dead bodies here in two days. That seems a little suspicious to me, Josie."

Millie fisted her hands on her hips. "Now that's technically not true. The first one was a skeleton and he was put in there years ago, nothing to do with any of us here. If you keep twisting the truth like that, Seth Chamberlain, I won't bake you that apple pie I promised for the town celebration."

Seth's eyes twinkled and he looked at Millie fondly, but I could tell the threat of her withholding the apple pie was real. "You might be right, but still that doesn't negate the fact that bodies seem to keep showing up at the guesthouse ever since you sold it to Josie."

Meow!

Nero, who had trotted over to join us earlier, voiced his disagreement. Good kitty. He and Marlowe were now sitting on their haunches in our circle and it appeared as if they were listening intently to everything we were saying.

"All right, I guess we will have to talk to each one of you and see if I can piece together Bob's activities last night." Seth walked over to take a closer look at the body. "Josie, you didn't notice that he didn't come in? Looks like he's been here all night."

"No, like I said, I was preparing the breakfast and then I went to bed early. I don't know what time people came and went."

Seth glanced over at the Biddefords. "Anyone see Bob last night?"

"Bob's an adult. We don't keep track of him," Carla said.

"Besides, we were all too busy minding our own business and looking for our own treasure," Arlene added.

"I might've seen something." *Hiccup*. Paula weaved on her feet.

Seth turned to face her. The look on his face told me he wasn't going to put much stock into what she had to say and, frankly, I couldn't blame him. I mean I *had* seen her sleeping in the bushes yesterday so she must have been soused.

"What did you see?" Seth asked.

She fidgeted. "Well, from the angle I was positioned in, it's kind of hard to say."

"Angle? Where were you?"

Her cheeks flushed and she pointed back toward the trail. "I was tired, so I took a little rest on that stone bench at the beginning of the trail that leads down here."

"On the bench?" Arlene snorted. "I think I saw you *under* the bench."

Paula straightened. "I might've taken a little nap but that doesn't mean I didn't see anything. You can see things from laying on the ground as easy as you can from sitting on the bench."

"Okay, so out with it. What did you see?" asked Seth.

"Well, I mean, it woke me up. I was a little groggy and down at that level you see different things." She glanced over at the body. "My memory is fuzzy but I'm sure I saw someone coming from the direction of the pond."

"Who?" Doris asked as the Biddefords eyed each other with suspicion.

Paula paused dramatically. I think she was enjoying the attention. Given the fact that she was probably drunk most of the time this might have been one of the few occasions anyone paid any notice to what she had to say. "That maid. You know, the one who doesn't really clean anything."

"Flora?" Millie looked at her incredulously. "Little short thing with round glasses?"

Paula crossed her arms over her chest and nodded emphatically. "Yep, that's the one. I saw her coming right down this path and she was walking pretty fast as if she was rushing away from the scene of a crime."

Chapter Twelve

Seth made everyone go back to the house. The Biddefords settled into the parlor and I brought them some tea and cookies. The Biddeford siblings didn't appear overly upset seeing as they'd just lost their brother. Doris, on the other hand, was appropriately distraught. She kept wringing her hands and wailing about her baby. Paula did her best to comfort her mother.

Mom and Millie hung out in the kitchen with Mike. Millie was irate that Seth would even consider suspecting Flora. Speaking of which, where was Flora? I hadn't seen her all morning.

The cats had followed us into the house and were settled in Millie and Mike's laps.

"Sunshine, are you okay?" Mike placed Marlowe down on the floor much to the chagrin of the cat and came over to stand next to me.

"Of course I'm okay. I'm not some delicate flower like Stella Dumont who needs a man to coddle me." Maybe my words came out a little sharper than I meant them, but I was a grown woman who had already proven that she was self-sufficient. And truth was I was still upset over how Mike had insisted I shouldn't investigate the last time we found a body. It was as if he thought I wasn't competent. Well, the joke was on him because I'd figured out who the killer was last time and I could do it again.

"Now I know what you girls are thinking." He looked over at Mom and Millie then glanced back at me. "There's no sense for you to go investigating this on your own. Murderers are dangerous."

See? I knew he was going to say that! Mom and I exchanged an eye-roll.

"Dangerous schmangerous." Millie jumped up from her seat. "Someone has accused Flora and I won't stand for it. She's practically family and has been here as long as I can remember. And she's a good, hard-working woman with dozens of grandchildren!"

Mike glanced at me as if looking for help. I shook my head. "If I feel like investigating, I'm going to."

"I'm a trained investigator, guys," Mike said. "If you want to investigate something you can ask me to do it for you. But we really should all leave the investigating to the police."

"I don't think we need you to do our dirty work for us." I glanced at Mom and Millie, who nodded.

"We've investigated plenty," Mom said.

"Yeah, what do you think we were doing while you were still in the navy?" Millie asked. "Got a pretty good track record, too, don't we, Rose?"

"Yeah, *we* know what we're doing. Josie here is the amateur," Mom said.

"Hey!" I bristled at her comment. Had she forgotten that I'd figured out who killed the last guest who had turned up dead? Sometimes nothing I did was good enough for my mother.

Seth appeared in the doorway and Millie scowled at him, taking the tray of cookies she had brought over from the counter and putting them away for emphasis.

"Have you seen Flora?" Seth asked.

"She's probably cleaning, as is her duty." Millie's posture was stiff and she avoided eye contact. "Now you know that nice little old lady couldn't have killed anyone."

Seth appeared visibly upset that Millie was cross with him. His sad gaze flicked to the cookies. His voice softened. "Now, Millie, you know I need to follow all the rules. I just want to question her."

"Question who?" Flora appeared in the doorway that led up the back stairs with a mop in her hand.

"I was just looking for you, Flora," Seth said.

"Oh, really? What for, Sheriff?" She looked around, noticing the grim looks on our faces. "What's going on?"

"Someone was killed on the grounds last night," Millie said.

Flora's brows shot up, her eyes getting even bigger behind her round glasses. She looked genuinely surprised, not that I had suspected her for a minute. "Really? Again?"

"I'm afraid so. Whacked over the head." Mom's comment earned a look of reproach from both Millie and Seth.

"I didn't see nothing." Flora opened the closet to put the mop away.

"Where were you last night?" Seth asked.

Flora turned and scowled at him. "What do you mean? I was at home."

"Are you sure you weren't here . . . Maybe digging for treasure?"

Flora's eyes flicked from Seth to Mom to Millie.

"Digging? I already told you I didn't see anything, what does it matter where I was?" She thrust her scrawny left arm, bent it at the elbow to make a muscle, and pointed to it with her right hand. "Does this look like an arm that could hit someone over the head hard enough to kill them?"

Seth looked at Flora uneasily. "Well, it's hard to say."

Flora rolled her eyes. "I don't have time for this." She looked at Mike. "Surely you don't think I killed someone, do you, Mr. Mike?"

As if to show their support, the cats ran over to Flora. She bent down to pet them, her knees popping and creaking. They sniffed her shoes gingerly, then rubbed their faces against her old wrinkled hands.

"Of course not, Flora. They don't have any concrete evidence against you, do you, Sheriff?" asked Mike.

Seth sighed. "No evidence. Just that someone saw her there."

"And who might that be?" Flora demanded.

"I can't really give out my sources," Seth stammered.

"Oh, come on. We all heard her say it." Millie turned to Flora. "It was Paula."

"The lush?" Flora waved her hand in the air. "She's not reliable. I've got things to clean. When you guys have something concrete then maybe you could come and arrest me, Seth. But don't forget I used to change your diapers and I've got stories to tell." Flora grabbed a roll of paper towels from under the sink and shuffled off upstairs.

I remembered Arlene's comments about the cleaning, so I called after her, "Could you double back into Earl and Arlene's room and make sure it's extra clean?"

She whirled around and scowled at me. I figured she was going to say she doesn't clean rooms, but instead she said, "What do you mean double back? Isn't that the green room?"

"Yes."

"Well, for your information, I haven't cleaned that one yet. If I had, it would be clean. I can only do one or two rooms a day, so I haven't gotten to the green room yet. But I will." She turned and we heard the stairs creaking as she went up.

"There you have it, Seth. Are you satisfied? Flora didn't do it. Now why don't you go try to dig up a real suspect," Millie said.

Seth stared at Millie with his sad eyes for a second, then he turned to Mike. "I'm ready to take your statement." As he and Mike started out of the room, Seth glanced over his shoulder at us. "Don't run off. I'll take all your statements but Mike's first. I'm sure he has to get back to work."

"Yes, I'm sure he does have to get back to work. He doesn't need to hang around here and *help* us," I said.

"Nope, we can help ourselves," Millie added, then under her breath, "And find the real killer even if the cops can't."

Mike shook his head and followed Seth out of the room.

Millie watched them leave then she opened the box of cookies and put them in front of us. We all took one. Snickerdoodles. "I had just baked these at home when I heard the police call on my scanner app. Lucky thing I thought to bring them. We might need them for sustenance. We need to get on top of this investigation before Flora gets into trouble." She glanced at the doorway. "Those men think they know everything. We'll show them."

I bit into my cookie. "Yeah, we're good at investigating. Do you think it has something to do with the treasure? Maybe Bob really did find it and someone killed him to take it away." Had there been a treasure buried in this yard the whole time I'd been struggling to pay bills?

Millie scowled. "That's just a stupid rumor. There was no hole or signs of digging near Bob and, besides, the odds of treasure being here are pretty much nil."

"Then why were you guys out here digging last night?" I asked.

Mom and Millie laughed. "What else are we going to do? Besides, half the town was here, and it was fun seeing them all. People get up to shenanigans at night and we wanted to spy and eavesdrop." She looked at my mom, a mischievous glint in her eyes. "Did you see Myron and Stella Dumont?"

"Yeah, they looked pretty chummy over by that gazebo." Mom glanced at me. "That should put your mind at ease, Josie."

I frowned. "Why is that?"

Mom rolled her eyes. "A blind monkey could see that you have a thing for Mike. I know you're still smarting about how he dumped you for Stella in high school, but it's time to get over that now. You're a grown woman with a daughter of your own and if Stella's chummy with Myron that means Mike is free pickings."

I closed my eyes and sighed. I wished my mom wouldn't try to fix me up. It was embarrassing at my age.

"I don't have a thing for Mike." Okay, maybe a little thing. I had to admit, even though his constant use of my childhood nickname bugged the crap out of me, he was kind of cute and the way he seemed concerned about me did make my heart flip-flop sometimes, but the last thing on my mind was striking up a relationship, Stella Dumont or not. "I think we need to focus on finding out who killed Bob, don't you?"

"Yeah. That's more fun than your love life," Millie said.

"I agree." Mom dug a cookie out of the box. "Now, who do you think did it?"

"It's got to be one of the family members. Did you see how Doris was the only one who seemed upset when we found him?" Millie asked.

"They don't get along very well," I said.

"And it's no wonder, what with them working with cheese all those years. That would make anyone not get along," Millie said.

"Bind you right up, too." Mom patted her stomach and made a face.

"You ask me, I think it was that drunk one, Paula." Millie leaned forward and lowered her voice. "I heard Bob threatening her the other day."

"You did? About what?" I asked.

"Something about her being a detriment to the company. Turns out her cheese sculptures are getting messed up because of her drinking. I overheard them arguing when we were outside digging last night. He said she should be fired from the company."

"And she's the one who put the finger on Flora. She might be trying to frame Flora to throw the police off track," Mom said.

"That would make sense, but I heard Bob arguing with someone, too," I said. "Carla."

"About what?" Millie asked.

"I'm not exactly sure. Bob said he wasn't going to stand for 'it' and she needed to make it right...or else."

"That sounds threatening," Millie said.

"Even worse, Henry overheard them and when he questioned Carla about it, she said for him not to worry about Bob because she was going to *do something about him*."

Mom munched on another cookie. "I wonder if *doing something* entailed killing him."

"Yeah, what if it did?" I said. "Thing is, it seems like the cheese company isn't doing very well and they're all blaming each other. It could've been any of them."

"Yeah, but now we have two suspects who we heard arguing with the victim. And we can do something that Seth can't do." Millie snapped off a bite of the cookie. "We can interview them one-on-one and try to trip them up so they confess."

Mom smiled and nodded. "Yeah, that sounds like fun. I say we start right away."

*

Nero sat under the kitchen table and aimed his gaze at Josie, willing her to understand his attempts at communication. Unfortunately, she was more interested in the conversation she was having with her mother and Millie about the suspect list.

"Doesn't matter how hard you stare at her, she's never going to be able to read your mind. Humans are just not that advanced," Marlowe said.

Nero sighed and trotted over to his favorite spot near the pantry where Millie had put two plush cat beds. He hopped into the blue one and curled up. "I know, but I wish we could tell them that we overheard Earl and Bob arguing."

"Then they could add Earl to their suspect list." Marlowe hopped up onto the counter. The humans weren't paying any attention, so she trotted over to the sink and tilted her head under the faucet to catch a drip of water. Fresh water out of the tap always tasted so delicious it was worth the risk of getting swatted at. "We'll just have to figure out a way to clue them in so that they get the idea into their heads on their own."

"But how? We can't *show* them an argument. We'll have to find something that points to Earl." Nero licked his front paw. "And we need to enlist the aid of the others to skulk around town keeping their eyes open for anything suspicious and listening in on conversations. The killer could be anyone who was here last night."

"Plenty of suspects on that roster." Marlowe jumped down from the counter and hopped into the tan cat bed beside Nero. "Do you think this has anything to do with the confession Juliette heard? She said something about a woman who was going to betray her family. Perhaps Millie's theory about Paula being the killer is correct."

"Well, it could be. I know one thing, though, it's not Flora. She's like family and we'll protect her like we would protect Millie," Nero said.

"Sure, but her shoes did smell kind of funny just now."

"But they didn't smell like murder. More smoke."

"Maybe she stepped in some cheese? A little slice of smoked Gouda. I think I saw Carla bring some into her room."

"Flora could have come into contact with it while cleaning, but we'll inspect their rooms thoroughly later today when they are out. Perhaps there will be some cheese morsels we can appropriate for ourselves. Purely for investigative purposes, of course. We would never steal from the guests," Nero said.

"Of course."

"Naturally, we must protect the reputation of the guesthouse and make sure the blame for this does not fall onto Josie or Flora. I wouldn't put it past that Seth Chamberlain to try to accuse one of them," Nero said.

"Ah, come on. We know Seth isn't that bad. He feeds us doughnut holes when no one else is looking."

"Exactly. That's what he does when no one is looking but right now everyone will be looking to see that he solves this case and there is an eyewitness pointing the finger at Flora. If he takes the easy way out, he could throw Flora in jail."

Marlowe nodded. "We need to help Millie, Rose and Josie figure out how to point him in another direction."

"Preferably not Josie's, though." Nero winced as Millie scraped her chair back. It made an ungodly noise, at least to his sensitive cat ears. It didn't seem to bother the humans any, though.

Millie went to the recipe box on the counter and started to leaf through the recipes. That meant baking. Well, fine. The humans could leisurely sit around baking all day but Nero didn't have that luxury. A killer was loose and he had to help catch them. He stood and stretched.

"Come on. Let's go down to the bait wharf and get this investigation rolling."

Chapter Thirteen

"Just how do you propose we interrogate the family?" my mother asked Millie, who was pawing through the recipes looking for the perfect one for the town celebration. Unfortunately, I hadn't had the presence of mind to hide the remains of my burned peanut-butter-banana loaf, and Millie had seen it in the trash.

Millie had her lips pressed together and was squinting at the cards as she flipped through them. She stopped and then pulled one out. "Yes, this is the one, the apple-pecan bread." She looked at me and nodded, her eyes sparkling. "That's the one, Josie. It's a showstopper. Now let me see if we have the ingredients."

She bustled over to the cabinets, pulling out the flour, sugar, baking soda, salt, a bag of pecans and a bottle of vanilla vodka. She had pulled some apples and a pitcher of orange juice out of the fridge, then turned to me. "Do you have any champagne?"

"Champagne and vodka?" my mother asked. "Do you put those in the apple-pecan bread?"

"No. Those are for Paula. I think she's making up that story about seeing Flora, and what better way to trip her up than to get her drunk?" Millie said. "And we all know she likes her drinks. I was thinking maybe we could cut her from the herd, serve her a complimentary vanilla mimosa and get her to confess."

It sounded like a good plan to me, and, luckily, I did have some champagne on hand in the butler's pantry. I knew one little drink wasn't going to loosen Paula's tongue much, so I proceeded to make a pitcher of mimosas. I might've taken a little sip or two for myself. I needed to steady my nerves. After all, it was a bit disconcerting that another body had shown up on the property.

Seth Chamberlain was taking people's statements in the reading room. He had the pocket doors shut, and, try as we might, we couldn't hear much through them.

"They sure don't make things like they used to. These doors are solid," Mom said as we pressed our ears to the door.

"Yeah, too bad," Millie added. "Oh well, let's find Paula, that will be much more enlightening than eavesdropping on Seth's investigation."

We found Paula sitting alone in the back parlor. The back parlor was a cozy room with overstuffed chairs and pillows in blue-and-yellow accents. Mike had painted the walls pale yellow and I'd had the pine floors refinished so they glowed like warm honey. The room wasn't used much because it didn't exactly have a nice view right now as it overlooked the gardens, which were an overgrown mess of tangles. Eventually, I would spruce them up, but now it was mostly weeds and dead flowers. Paula didn't seem to mind, though. She was sitting in the chair, her blank gaze fixed at something outside the window.

Perhaps her somber mood was due to guilt over

killing her brother and she'd break down and confess right away. That would be convenient for me, avoiding a long, drawn-out investigation with the police traipsing through my guesthouse.

"That dreadful sheriff has already taken my statement. It was so stressful." Paula lifted a shaky cup of tea to her lips.

"I know, dear," Millie clucked and sat down beside her. I set the silver tray with the pitcher and a champagne flute on the table beside Millie, and she poured a mimosa and held it out to Paula. "We've prepared a little something for you to settle your nerves."

Paula's eyes lit up. She grabbed the glass, settled back into the chair and chugged the whole thing down.

"Would you like another?" Millie asked.

Paula nodded and Millie topped the glass off.

"It must've been dreadful for you, dear, seeing your brother like that," Millie said.

Paula nodded, the glass still to her lips.

"Funny that you were right at the beginning of that trail last night, though. I don't think a lot of people were down there digging for treasure, so what made you think that would be a good place to dig?" I asked.

"I didn't. I went there because it was out of the way. I didn't want to be disturbed, that's why I chose that particular bench," Paula said.

"But it seems odd that you would've seen Flora down there. I mean, like we said, it was out of the way and I don't even think she was digging for treasure. Are you sure it was her?" Millie asked. "I mean, she is kind of old to be traipsing around out there at night."

Paula put the glass down and wrung her hands together. "I know. That's what the sheriff said. I got the impression he thinks I made that up, but I swear I didn't kill Bob, and I'm sure it was the maid I saw."

"But you did have a fight with Bob earlier, didn't you?" I asked.

Paula's eyes narrowed. "What makes you say that?"

"Oh, somebody else mentioned it. I think it was something about your cheese sculptures not being up to par."

Paula sniffed. "Sure, we fought about that, but that was nothing new. Bob was always fighting with us about one thing or another, and that's no reason to kill him. I really was on that bench asleep, honest."

"So Flora woke you up when she came by then? Was she carrying a shovel?" I'd looked at the back of Bob's head and was pretty sure that he'd been hit with a shovel, but I hadn't seen any blood on the shovel at the crime scene. I glanced out the window in time to see Johnnie collecting the shovels from the shed. Looked like I was right then.

Paula closed her eyes as if trying to remember. "You know, I'm not sure if she had a shovel, but I saw her clear as day coming down that path. She didn't notice me because I was on the ground out of the line of sight."

I jumped on the inconsistency in Paula's description. "Well, if you were lying on the ground asleep like you said you were, then how could you see Flora coming down the path? You must've been awake to see her."

She squinted again and sipped her mimosa. "Right. Something else woke me up because I did see Flora, but after I was jolted awake by something."

"Some*thing* or some*one*?" Millie asked.

Paula took a deep breath. "I guess it was someone. Someone stepped on my hand. I didn't see who it was, though. I was fast asleep on the ground, my face pressed to the grass, and then all of a sudden, there was this big shooting pain in my hand." She made a face and winced, grabbing her hand. "I woke up right away, but the person had already gone by. All I remember seeing is a black Ferragamo tag on the back of their shoes, then when I turned back to try to pull myself up, I saw the maid coming down the path."

"Ferragamo shoes?" Millie raised her brows. "Those are very expensive shoes. Not everyone wears those."

"Yeah, and what kind of a moron would wear them digging in the dirt?" my mother asked.

Paula's eyes widened as if she had made a sudden realization. "I know one moron who would. My brother, Earl."

*

I went to the kitchen to wash out the empty mimosa pitcher while Mom and Millie ran off to find Seth so they could tell him about the Ferragamo shoes.

If Paula was telling the truth and she really was asleep at the time, I was sure she hadn't been simply napping. She'd been passed out drunk, which made her an incredibly unreliable witness. I still wasn't convinced that she wasn't making the whole thing up so she could frame someone because she was the real killer. Maybe she figured she could throw the investigation off track by implicating both Flora *and* Earl.

On my way back to the parlor I passed the front sitting room and saw poor Doris in there looking as if she'd lost her best friend. My heart squeezed. The woman's son had just been murdered and it was possible that one of her other kids did it.

I slipped into the sitting room. "Can I bring you something? Maybe some tea? I have some fresh snickerdoodle cookies."

So what if I didn't mention that Millie had baked them at her house? Did it really matter where they'd come from? If Doris thought I had nicely baked cookies for her and gave me a good review on Yelp because of it, Millie wouldn't mind my little lapse.

Doris turned red-rimmed eyes to me, then glanced in the direction of the kitchen, her nose twitching. "Are they burning?"

I straightened my back. See what happened when you were nice? People mocked you.

"No." I wasn't baking anything so of course nothing was burning.

She sighed and slumped in the chair. "It's just so awful, that Sheriff interrogating us. It's preposterous to think one of us would have murdered Bob."

"Do you know anyone who *would* have wanted to murder him?" I wasn't pumping the grieving mother for information, just trying to take her mind off things. But if she happened to have some information about who might have wanted Bob dead, all the better.

Doris pressed her lips together. "Hopefully not his own brother or sisters, though there has been a lot of fighting and animosity lately. You see, Bob could be a bit of a troublemaker. Never quite got along with the rest of the family."

I raised my brows. Maybe Bob had done something to his brother or sisters and they had a long festering animosity toward him. "Really? What kind of trouble?"

Doris shrugged. "You know, the usual things. Not pulling his weight. Wanting to surf and ski instead of working. Marrying that awful woman."

I frowned. Bob hadn't brought a wife to the guest-house. "He was married?"

"Yep. They were getting a divorce. Good riddance to her, I say."

"Is it an amicable divorce?" My hopes rose. Maybe the person who had killed Bob was his soon-to-be ex-wife.

Doris wiggled her hand back and forth in a seesaw motion. "So-so. I guess it's fairly friendly, as divorces go."

I inched forward to the edge of my chair. "You don't think the ex-wife could have killed him, do you?"

"I wish. It would take the heat off my other children. I can tell that the sheriff suspects them." Doris looked thoughtful, as if she was coming to terms with the possibility that one of her children had killed Bob. "But she's out of the country. I told the sheriff all about her. He's going to double-check, but, honestly, I wouldn't think she'd have it in her."

"What about somebody else from his past? If he was a troublemaker, maybe he rubbed someone the wrong way."

"Bob rubbed a lot of people the wrong way, but I have no idea who he would have angered so much that they'd come here to kill him. I don't think he knows anyone from Oyster Cove and most of the people he associates with are losers who wouldn't travel so far to do him in." Doris shook her head. "It's just such bad timing with the family tensions being high because the business is doing so badly."

"I'm sorry," I said, not knowing what else to say.

"I suppose I'll have to arrange a funeral. If only the cheese-sculpting business was doing better we could do something more lavish, but I guess now it will have to be something simple," Doris said.

I patted her hand for comfort. "Simple is better, sometimes."

Doris nodded. "They're not bad children, you know. Even though they each have their little quirks. I blame my husband for making them so lazy and selfish. He wanted them to have it easier than we did and didn't want them to work as hard. Barney and I started the business from scratch, you know."

"You don't say. What made you start a cheese-sculpting business?" I asked.

Doris smiled at the memory. "Barney used to make little sculptures out of cheese for parties and all our friends loved them. It was just a silly hobby, but then people started asking if they could order specific sculptures. Next thing we knew, we were shipping out of state and running a full-blown business." Doris swiped at the tears drying on her cheeks. "When the kids were grown, we brought them in, and when Barney died they took over. Sometimes when you get something for nothing, you don't appreciate it. You don't work as hard. I've used up all my retirement income supplementing the business."

I nodded. I knew how that was. I'd worked my whole marriage to make things good for my husband and he hadn't appreciated it one bit. I'd put my whole life savings into the guesthouse and my future depended on its success. I sure as heck was going to work my butt off and not let it fall to ruin like Doris's cheese-sculpting business. All the more reason to clear up this murder fast. I'd do just about anything to make sure my business was a success.

Hey, wait a minute…hadn't Doris mentioned spending her retirement income earlier in reference to the treasure? She'd looked pretty serious too. But surely she wouldn't bash her own son over the head in order to grab the treasure from him?

"Of course, some of them don't have a lick of sense and that might be part of it. Take Carla, for example." Doris shook her head and looked out the window. "Now before we started digging, we discussed where the old homestead was located in Jedediah's day. Even though he started off with a pretty big house, it's been added to quite a bit over the years. Carla knew the gazebo didn't exist on the grounds back then, it was added after Millie's people bought it."

I nodded. Apparently talking had comforted her. She was more animated and not as sad now. "I'm going to have that restored, the gazebo."

"Good idea, but Carla should have been smarter. See, that's why the business is failing." Doris tapped her head with her forefinger. "They don't use their smarts."

"Why do you say that?"

"Because last night when we were digging, I saw Carla coming from the gazebo. Now we know Jedediah wouldn't bury treasure there because there was nothing there in his day. No trees, no landmarks, nothing, and everyone knows, when you bury treasure, you need a landmark so you can locate it later."

I thought about that. Why would Carla be digging in a place unlikely to have treasure? Did she know something the others didn't? The gazebo wasn't near the pond, but could she have killed Bob at the pond, then taken a long route to get away? Maybe she'd gotten lost in the overgrown bushes and grasses and found her way out at the gazebo.

A ruckus in the hallway interrupted my thoughts.

"That's preposterous. Who would wear fine Italian leather shoes to go digging in the yard?" It was Earl. Millie had obviously talked to Seth, who was questioning him about the shoes.

"Who knows what people wear to dig? Now answer the question. Do you have Ferragamo shoes?" Seth said.

"Yes, but I was wearing Nikes," Earl said, "and I can prove it."

Doris and I went into the hallway in time to see Earl stomping up the stairs. We heard him rip open his door, then slam it shut loudly.

We all stood around looking at each other.

"What's this about?" Doris asked.

"Your daughter Paula seems to think she saw fancy Ferragamo shoes when she was passed out on the bench before Flora ran past," Millie said.

Doris scrunched up her face. "Are you people colluding? Trying to get my daughter to say something that she didn't really see? I mean, you know she's not that reliable." Doris made nip-tipping gestures with her thumb and forefinger against her lips.

"I'm just being thorough," Seth assured her. He narrowed his eyes at Millie. "We won't be playing favorites here."

After what seemed like ages, Earl came running down the stairs with a pair of white Nikes in his hand. He threw them down on the round table in the foyer so hard that the Tiffany bird lamp with the delicate stained-glass shade wobbled precariously. I cringed as I pictured the dirt in between the treads caking off onto Millie's grandmother's hand-tatted white doily.

"See?" Earl pointed at the mud caked on the side of his shoes. "Those are the shoes I was wearing last night, so if my sister claims she saw someone with Ferragamo shoes walking past her, then it wasn't me."

Chapter Fourteen

The pungent smell of dead fish tickled Nero's nostrils as he came around the side of the harbormaster's station.

"Ah, we're in luck. They've got fish scraps." Marlowe picked up speed. Likely, she wanted to get to the others before the scraps were gone.

The other cats were already hunkered down near the lobster traps. Poe was chowing down on a halibut head. Juliette was finishing off a haddock tail. Stubbs was industriously picking clean the bones of a cod. Boots must have just finished eating and was now fastidiously preening his whiskers.

As Nero approached, a gull swooped down and attempted to steal a piece of fish away from Harry. Harry hung on with one claw. "Hey, give it back."

Caw!

The gull flapped its wings with its beak deep into the morsel of fish.

Harry tugged. The gull pulled back.

"That's mine, go get your own." Harry tried to grab at the fish with both paws but the gull was stronger. He ripped the meat out of Harry's paw and flew off. Nero could have sworn the gull's cry sounded like "ha ha!"

"Stupid gulls. They're a nuisance." Harry sat back on his haunches and preened.

"I agree." Juliette pushed a piece of her haddock over to Harry.

Stubbs finished picking the last bit off the bones of his cod and tossed a perfectly formed fish skeleton into the water, then looked at Nero. "So, what's going on? You guys figure out who plugged the vic?"

"He wasn't plugged," Nero said. "He was bludgeoned with a shovel."

"Hit from behind," Marlowe added.

"From behind? So it wasn't a fight, then?" Boots's green eyes brimmed with curiosity. "Do you think they got him by surprise?"

"Good question. Someone could have snuck up on him, I suppose, or maybe he knew the person and wasn't afraid to turn his back. I don't see how that narrows it down much, though."

"It could have been one of his siblings; he was on the outs with all of them," Marlowe said.

"Have you located the shovel that was used as the murder weapon yet?" Harry asked.

Nero shook his head. "It could be anywhere."

"That makes our job harder. Almost everyone in town was out there last night with a shovel." Boots tugged at his whiskers. "But you said you heard the victim argue with someone?"

"Several people," Nero said. "Marlowe and I heard him argue with Earl."

"And Josie heard him arguing with Carla. Josie claims that Carla even made a threatening comment about him," Marlowe added.

"And Millie heard him arguing with Paula," Nero said.

"What were they arguing about?" Juliette asked.

"Seems like it all stems from their cheese-sculpting business. It's not doing well. It seems Bob had made threats to each of them."

"What kind of threats?" Stubbs asked.

"It would appear Bob had something on them and might have been about to expose what he knew."

The cats looked pensive. Everyone knew that mixing family with business was fraught with danger, especially if that business was having problems.

"Sounds like tempers might have been high. And maybe someone didn't want Bob to make good on his threats," Harry said.

"Bob was the most disruptive one, maybe Doris did him in so they could have harmony in the company again?" Marlowe suggested.

Juliette hissed. "The mother? I don't think a mother would kill one of her kits. Not unless there was something wrong with it."

"Sounds like there was plenty wrong with this Bob character," Harry said.

"Yeah, it's the age-old motive. Silence anyone who might drop the dime on you or is getting in the way of something you really want," Stubbs agreed.

Poe picked a piece of fish out of his teeth with a razor-sharp claw. "In any case, I think we should be able to get some cheese samples out of this job. Maybe a pinch of Parmesan or a wedge of Wensleydale or a morsel of mozzarella."

Juliette frowned at him. "Mozzarella? Do you think

they would have that? I don't think you can sculpt mozzarella. It's not firm enough."

"But it is delicious."

"True." Juliette smacked her lips together. "Maybe with some little tomatoes and basil or—"

"Kids," Nero cut in. "Let's stick to the question at hand. What course of action should we take to ferret out the killer? As you heard, our dear friend Flora has been accused by one of the siblings and of course we must make sure this doesn't reflect badly on Josie."

"We all know Flora could not have committed such a heinous crime," Boots said.

"Surely Seth Chamberlain won't think it's Josie again? She has no motive," Stubbs added.

Juliette jumped on top of the lobster traps. She often liked to get up higher than the rest so she could look down upon them, especially when she thought she had information that she considered to be important. "Don't forget, I heard the woman confessing about betraying her family. I believe that could have been the killer trying to clear her conscience before committing the crime."

"Do you think you would be able to recognize her voice? Was she one of the siblings at the crime scene earlier?" Nero asked.

Juliette shook her head. "In the confessional people whisper so you can't recognize the tone that way. But it does narrow our suspect list down to a woman."

"Who confesses to a murder before they commit it?" Stubbs asked. "The confession could have been about something else. I don't want to narrow down the list prematurely."

Juliette gave him a haughty look and jumped down off the lobster trap. "Fine, then *you* come up with a plan."

"I have a plan," Nero said. "I want you all to canvas the town. Sniff out all the shovels, see if you can find the murder weapon among them. The cops took the shovels from the Oyster Cove Guesthouse toolshed, but only the Biddefords used those shovels. If the killer is someone else, the shovel could be hidden somewhere around town."

"Yeah, we can't forget that the guesthouse grounds were lousy with diggers last night. Anyone could have whacked him," Stubbs said.

"Poe, Stubbs, Boots, you check around the alleys and benches downtown. See if you can overhear anything or pinpoint guilty behavior. Harry, get the word out to your network that we are looking for the killer." Harry was a scrappy street cat with a network of informants that would rival any cable network.

Harry nodded.

"Juliette, you stick close to the confessional at the rectory in case our confessor comes back. If your theory is correct, they may need to cleanse their soul of the guilt."

Juliette swished her tail in agreement.

"Meanwhile, Marlowe and I will investigate the rooms at the guesthouse. If someone is hiding something there, we'll find it."

*

It was almost noon by the time Seth finished interviewing everyone and departed. Mom and Millie had left

me with the ingredients and instructions for the apple-
pecan bread and I had baked a trial loaf, which I left
cooling on the counter before meeting Mom and Millie downtown to make the final touches on the Oyster
Cove Guesthouse table at the town celebration. I hadn't
burned the cake this time, though it did smell a little bit
like sour cider. At least I was making progress.

The Biddefords were ambling around the guesthouse, talking in hushed tones. They seemed to be in
a somber mood again. I couldn't imagine one of them
had killed Bob, though the alternatives were also not
that great. It had either been one of them, someone
from town or Flora. Speaking of Flora, I hadn't seen
her since she'd talked to Seth in the kitchen, but that
didn't necessarily mean anything. It wasn't like she'd
skip town or anything.

The town common was full of activity again. This
time tourists were milling about, sampling the goods
here and picking up brochures there. This weekend
even more tents would be set up on the other side,
part of a gigantic craft fair after the parade. The mood
was festive, and maybe word about the murder hadn't
spread yet.

Stella Dumont was hovering around her table. She
wore a tight V-neck shirt and a pound of makeup, and
was meticulously fussing with her brochures, arranging
them just so and standing back to admire the presentation. I glanced back at my table where my brochures lay
in a messy pile. I sauntered over and started arranging
them, peeking surreptitiously at Stella to see how she
was doing hers.

"No copying. Just like in high school, Josie," Stella said.

"I wasn't copying." Where were Mom and Millie? They had requested I meet them here and I hoped they'd hurry so I didn't have to talk to Stella for too long.

"You're always after the things I have. Like Mike," Stella said.

I crossed my arms over my chest. "I heard you were after Myron now."

Stella's brows knit together and she laughed then continued fussing with her brochures.

"I think *you're* after what *I* have now," I said.

Stella paused what she was doing and looked up at me. "What do you mean?"

"I saw you in my yard digging for treasure last night," I said. Technically that wasn't correct. I hadn't seen her in my yard, just scoping it out. But Millie had said she'd seen Stella and Myron so I figured that was almost as good as seeing her there myself.

"Oh, that. I just wanted to see what the fuss was all about. Who believes there is still an old treasure there anyway? That's silly."

"Well, lots of the townspeople were there so apparently not everyone thinks it's silly," I said.

"People love to gamble. Look at how many play the lottery. People just came out because there was a *chance* there is treasure. I don't think too many actually believe in it." In the corner of the tent sat Myron, donning his perfectly pressed suit. He'd snagged a young couple and was pointing to something in one of his brochures. Trying to sell them a loan no doubt. "Even people who already have money can be lured by the dream of finding treasure—even if they don't deserve more."

What was that all about? She sounded mad at Myron. Had he given her the brush-off? She couldn't really be interested in him, could she? Maybe it was all his family money. Mike was a lot more handsome. Not that I was comparison shopping or anything.

Her words made me wonder. Why *would* Myron be out there digging when there was only a slim chance anything would be found? He wasn't the type to get his hands dirty and his family came from old money. Maybe the bank wasn't doing well...was that why they had a table here? The First Oyster Cove Bank and Trust didn't usually need to drum up business. It was the only bank around and everyone in town used them for their checking accounts, loans, investments and savings.

"How'd the bread come out?" Somehow Millie and Mom had snuck up and were standing beside me.

"Not too bad. At least I didn't burn it."

"That's good." She leaned in and lowered her voice. "And what about the suspects? Did anyone blurt out a confession?"

"Unfortunately, no. The closest we came was Earl with the shoes."

"Those shoes! Can you believe he put them down on Grandma Sullivan's tatted doily?" Millie glanced up at me. "Flora did clean that off, didn't she? I hope it doesn't stain."

I wondered about that. Flora cleaning it, I mean, not the staining. Flora had made herself scarce after talking to Seth in the kitchen and I couldn't really say I blamed her. It doesn't feel very good to be accused of killing someone—I should know.

I made a mental note to check on the doily as soon as I got home. Millie seemed distraught about it, so I wanted to make sure it got cleaned even if I had to do it myself.

"Actually, I haven't seen Flora since we talked with her and Seth this morning." I glanced over at the grand-mothers of twins' table, but Flora wasn't there. "She didn't say she was taking any time off, but she might have been busy cleaning when I left."

"Flora? I thought she'd be preparing for her trip." Annabel Drescher piped in from the table to our left. Clearly, she'd been eavesdropping.

The table was for the Drescher Travel Agency that Annabel owned. It was decorated in a turquoise-and-coral beachy theme, no doubt to entice innocent celebration-goers into buying one of their expensive Caribbean beach packages. Annabel was dressed to the nines as usual with a fancy tailored suit, understated but expensive jewelry, and what looked like a very expen-sive leather handbag resting next to her chair. Probably keeping it within arm's reach in case someone tried to make off with it. Naturally, the handbag matched the pair of designer shoes she had on her size-nine feet.

"Trip? What do you mean? Flora isn't going on a trip, is she, Josie?" My mom turned to me and I shook my head. That was the first I'd heard of any trip.

"Oh yes she is. She was in the travel agency asking about some coordinates." Annabel straightened some pamphlets.

"Coordinates?" Millie asked.

"Yeah, you know, longitude and latitude. She was a little bit off, though, because they ended up in the Caribbean Sea but I think she wanted the island of Martinique. At least, that's the package I'm gonna try to sell her," Annabel said.

"Did she say when she was going on this trip?" I asked. Flora hadn't mentioned any plans, which made me a little suspicious. What was going on with her? Of course, I couldn't imagine that she'd have killed Bob but where would Flora have gotten the money for a trip? She was always complaining about how hard it was to survive on Social Security and a maid's wages. As far as I knew, she was broke.

"You know she was a little vague about that when I asked. Said she'd have to come into a lot of money to afford it. But she must've been expecting some soon because why else would she be asking about a specific place?" Annabel shrugged and smiled, showing her ultra-white teeth, just like the ones Jaws showed right before he tried to eat the boat. "I don't try to force them. Whenever someone comes in with a hankering for a vacation I know sooner or later they're gonna buy."

I exchanged a glance with Mom and Millie. This was not looking good. Flora thought she might come into some money, Paula claimed to have seen her rushing away from the scene of the crime, and Flora had denied that. What if Seth's theory about Bob finding the treasure and someone killing him over it was true? And what if that someone really had been Flora?

I didn't have long to think about it because a voice boomed from behind us.

"Heard about the goings-on at your place!" We all spun around to see Myron Remington standing there looking superior. "Seems like you're racking up the bodies like nobody's business. Maybe you should get a loan for a new wing. A mortuary wing."

"I don't think that's anything to make jokes about, Myron," Millie said.

"No joke, actually. I really could give you a loan. I have some great rates right now and I'd love to see that old place fully restored."

I eyed him suspiciously and thought about taking on a loan. On the one hand, it would be great to get the house done in one fell swoop, instead of working on it a little at a time, but I was also maxed out on monthly bills. I couldn't pay the note on a loan no matter how good the interest rate was. "I'll think about it, Myron."

He nodded. "Hey, how is the investigation going on that skeleton? Did I hear it ended up being Jedediah Biddeford?"

"That's what Seth says, but there's not much of an investigation going on. My daughter pointed out we could have a forensic anthropologist look into the old bones. Might be able to tell us more." I couldn't help the tinge of pride that snuck into my voice at the mention of Emma's suggestion. Maybe I should suggest that idea to Seth, though not right now. In light of finding another body on my property, it would be best to steer clear of Seth Chamberlain and avoid making him feel like I was telling him how to do his job.

"That seems like it would be quite a waste, doesn't it?" Myron fiddled with his silk paisley tie. "You know how I hate wasting money."

"Well, it wouldn't actually be your money, Myron, but yes, it does seem like a waste," Millie said.

"Speaking of your money, did I hear you were in my yard trying to find the treasure last night?" I asked.

Myron looked taken aback. "Treasure? No. Why would I dig up treasure? I own a bank."

"So you weren't in my yard? With Stella Dumont?"

He looked sharply over at Stella's table and she turned her back on him. "I should certainly say not. I couldn't even get a shovel to dig up treasure if I wanted. Your maid Flora got the last one."

Chapter Fifteen

Since I was already in town, I figured I'd visit Jen. I'd been so busy lately that we'd rarely gotten a chance to talk. I wanted to catch up. Okay, I admit that I had an ulterior motive. The post office was rumor central and I wanted to get some insider information on what people were saying about the murder.

Jen was standing about five feet from the open slots on the postmaster side of the post-office boxes with a stack of letters in her hand. She was oblivious to the fact that someone had come in, her concentration aimed at pitching each letter into its rightful post-box slot like she was practicing for darts.

Thwack. Thwack. Thwack. Each letter made a hollow sound as it slid, hitting the slot door on the other side.

She noticed me as I approached the desk because she stopped pitching and turned, her mouth quirking in a smile.

"Oh, thank goodness. Someone to talk to. It gets so boring in here and I have to make up little games to keep myself amused." She gestured toward the post-office boxes. "So, what's up?"

"I just came down to check out my table under the tent. Millie is obsessing about having a good presentation."

Jen's face turned serious and she reached out and patted my forearm, which I had rested on the counter. "I heard about the murder. Are you okay?"

"Sure. Never let a little thing like murder in my guesthouse get me down. I might be getting used to it."

"Well, let's hope it doesn't become a common occurrence." Jen's concerned eyes turned inquisitive. "Any idea who did it?"

I glanced around to make sure we really were alone. The post office had a lot of nooks and crannies and you never knew where someone might be lurking around reading the magazines or fliers they'd gotten before tossing them in the recycling bins. No one was around. "I think it might be one of his siblings. Can you believe one of them tried to pin it on Flora?" I said.

"Flora? No way." Her eyes narrowed. "Do you think that person was trying to divert suspicion away from themselves?"

"Possibly." I picked a candy out of the bowl that sat on top of the counter. Hershey's Kisses. If I had that on my counter the bowl would be empty in about five minutes. "What are people saying?"

Jen shot me a mischievous look. "First tell me what's going on with you and Mike. I heard he was the one who discovered the body so that means he must have been at your place very early this morning."

I rolled my eyes. My mother and Millie weren't the only ones meddling in my nonexistent love life. Jen had been wanting to see Mike and me get back together since I moved back to town. Not happening.

"Yes, he was there." I let my voice trail off and gave

her a coquettish look just to yank her chain. I almost felt bad at the hopeful gleam in her eye.

"I knew it! Did he stay over?"

I drew it out, popping another Hershey Kiss in my mouth and pretending to be too busy chewing to answer. Jen was practically jumping out of her black government-issued shoes with anticipation.

I swallowed and smiled. "Nah. He was just there to inspect the toolshed. That's why he was down near the pond."

"I heard it was in the pond. But you're sure he didn't fall in and drown on his own?"

"Nope. The back of his skull was crushed."

I gave her the *Reader's Digest* condensed version of finding the body and what had gone on this morning, with Seth interrogating people and how Paula had claimed to see Flora coming up the path from the pond.

"Flora? She wouldn't harm a fly. She's a great-grandmother, for crying out loud."

"I know." I pressed my lips together. Of course Flora wouldn't kill anyone. She was loyal, trustworthy and a good worker. Okay, scratch that part about a good worker. She was loyal and trustworthy, though. And I couldn't picture her bashing someone over the head with a shovel, especially with those scrawny arms of hers. But still, something didn't sit right. There were a few disturbing, unanswered questions when it came to Flora.

"She has been acting a little odd lately. Did you hear anything about her going on a trip?" I asked.

Jen shook her head. "But I wouldn't necessarily hear about that."

"True." Not everyone gave Jen their itinerary, though most people going on a trip had their mail stopped. Flora lived in an apartment and would probably have a neighbor or her landlord collect it. So, unless Flora was going with someone who might create a scandal, the post-office grapevine would find her trip uninteresting.

"Do they have any other suspects?" Jen peeled a stamp off a stamp sheet and pressed it onto an envelope, then tossed the envelope into a mailbag.

"I'm not sure. Seth probably suspects me, though."

Jen laughed. "What motive would you have?"

"None, but he was looking at me with suspicion. Remember he thought I killed the last person too."

"Only because you own the guesthouse now and were out of town for a long time and he thought you killed the last victim because he was going to give the guesthouse a bad review. But it really does come down to motive, doesn't it? I heard that Seth thought perhaps someone killed Bob to take the treasure away from him. Do you think he dug something up?" Jen asked.

"Did you hear anything about any treasure through the grapevine?" If someone had the treasure, chances were someone else knew about it and sooner or later that person would talk. I doubted there actually was any treasure, though, or that Bob had dug it up. If he had, wouldn't the hole—or at least evidence of digging it—have still been there?

"You don't really believe that whole treasure curse thing, do you?" Jen asked.

"No. You?"

"Nope. But some people do. I've heard a few people say that old Jedediah killed Bob to make good on his curse."

"If that were the case, then Bob would still have had the treasure in his possession. Unless they think a ghost took it away."

Jen laughed. "With some of the folks here, I wouldn't be surprised."

"No, I think this murder was done by someone on the earthly plane. Someone closer to the victim."

"You mean like his family?"

I nodded. "Bob had threatened several of them. The business isn't going well and apparently they were all at odds."

Jen nodded. "Typically the victim knows the killer." She watched a lot of crime shows on TV.

"You haven't heard any rumors about anyone in town knowing Bob from before, have you?"

Jen slapped another stamp on an envelope and tossed it in the bag. "Nope."

"Anyone come to town asking around for him? He's getting a divorce, but his wife is supposed to be in Europe."

Jen's left brow rose. "An estranged wife? Sounds like a person with a motive. Unfortunately, I haven't heard of anyone looking for him. The only people asking about the Biddefords are those interested in the skeleton you found. That seems to have raised everyone's curiosity. Even Myron Remington was in here asking about the investigation."

"He was asking me too, but Sheriff Chamberlain

isn't going to investigate Jedediah's death. I mean, how can he?"

"The clues are too old and a fresh murder would take priority, I imagine," Jen said. "Myron's family has history here. Maybe he was more interested in the historical aspect or maybe he's one of those creepy serial-killer ghouls who is fascinated with skeletons and bodies."

Jen had an excited look on her face as she said this. I started to worry that maybe she'd been watching *too many* crime shows.

"He always was a little weird. I think he might have only been feigning interest so he could make googly eyes at Stella Dumont."

"He was making googly eyes at Stella?" The dramatic look on Jen's face was replaced by skepticism.

"Millie said she saw them together last night on the grounds when everyone was digging."

Jen waggled her brows. "Together, together?"

The thought made my lips purse like I'd eaten a sour lemon. "Ugh…did you have to put that image in my head? I think they were just talking. She seemed to imply they were an item but then today Myron denied even being there. Said it was beneath his dignity and he had plenty of money already."

"Sounds like something he would say. He always acted superior especially since he went to a better college than the rest of us. Maybe his business isn't doing well and he needs an influx of money but doesn't want anyone to know. He always was worried about appearances."

"Or maybe he wanted to hide the fact he really was with Stella."

"Well, I wouldn't be surprised if Stella was trying to hook Myron. He has the money and you know how she likes to go for that."

"True."

"At least she won't be going for Mike if she's after Myron. Not that Mike would give her the time of day," Jen said slyly.

This time I didn't bite. "Well, I better get going. During the interrogations someone got Millie's grandmother's doily dirty and I want to make sure it's clean before I get home."

"Shouldn't Flora do that?" Jen asked.

I raised my eyebrows in response and she laughed. "Oh yeah, what was I thinking?" She picked up her big pile of envelopes as I turned to leave. "Well, one thing at least, you won't have to worry about people coming over to dig more holes in your yard tonight."

That was welcome news since I was starting to worry about how to control the hole diggers. I didn't need another one ending up dead. "Why is that?"

"Everyone is scared off because of the curse. I told you, a lot of folks think Jedediah Biddeford made good on his promise. They think he already killed one person digging up his treasure and no one else wants to be next."

Chapter Sixteen

"Searching rooms is exhausting," Nero said as he flopped down in a pool of sunshine in the conservatory.

"The actual searching is fun, but it's tedious timing things so precisely so that we can get in and out," Marlowe said. "I mean, waiting around until someone opens the door then darting inside without being noticed and then making sure we don't get trapped inside. Sneaking out when the door is open…"

"It's risky if we have to resort to the old meowing incessantly to go in and then out and then in again trick," Nero said.

"Good thing we know some secret passages in this old place."

"Too bad all our efforts were for nothing, though. We didn't find a thing."

"We did get to sample some of that Gouda Paula had in her room," Marlowe said. "Good thing Gouda doesn't need to be refrigerated. I would hate to have it mess with my digestion."

Nero shot Marlowe a recriminating look. "I think you got a little overzealous with that sculpture by the way. I hope she doesn't notice that the ears are missing from the smaller bunny."

Paula had made a sculpture of a grassy field with

rabbits. It was actually rather nice and the little blades of grass were perfect for nibbling without anyone noticing. Of course, Marlowe had to get greedy and go for one of the ears. Hopefully Paula would just think she'd bitten them in a drunken fog or maybe blame one of her siblings.

Marlowe turned away, appropriately embarrassed. "Perhaps I did get a bit carried away. I was frustrated that our search didn't turn up any evidence."

Nero had shown Marlowe some of his most valued methods of clue detection, yet they had not found anything. "At least Flora cleaned Earl and Arlene's room. That woman has been quite obnoxious about it."

"She sure was. I hope they find out that she's the killer. I don't like her at all," Marlowe said.

"I don't actually like many of the Biddefords. I mean, what kind of family argues all the time? Family should stick by each other, not be at each other's throats," Nero reflected. "I guess Doris is okay, but then I do have a fondness for older humans."

Marlowe trotted over to the potted ficus trees and started sniffing. "Hey, did you dig over here again? There's dirt all over the floor. Josie is not going to like that. Or did you do that on purpose to keep her in line?" Marlowe glanced over her shoulder at Nero.

Nero's whiskers twitched. What was the young cat talking about? He sighed and got up from his warm spot to see.

"I didn't dig here. If I was to spew dirt to keep Josie in line, I would make it much more obvious and spread it all over the room like this." Nero swatted at a large clump of dirt and it skidded out into the middle of the room breaking up into smaller pieces. "See, now that piece Josie would be able to see from the doorway. You need to be more obvious with these things."

"Me? I didn't mess with the dirt." Marlowe cocked her head and looked at one of the boarded-up windows. "I do think someone has been here, though."

They trotted over to the window and sniffed. "Smells like fresh wood and nails." Something in the corner caught Nero's eye and he snaked his paw out and batted it around. A shiny new nail.

"Ed must have been here. But why would he dig in the plant?"

"Beats me, but it looks like someone did. Maybe it was one of the guests."

"Either that or we've got another cat in here, and I think if we had another cat one of us would know."

Nero laughed. Of course his superior senses would have alerted them to an intruder cat.

"It is curious. Sadly, these humans must be dumber than I thought. Surely they aren't stupid enough to think the treasure is buried in a potted plant?"

Marlowe trotted over and lay in the sunny spot under the window. Curling her tail around her and closing her eyes she muttered, "Don't ask me, I wouldn't put anything past them. Maybe it wasn't one of them, maybe it was that dead guy's ghost. I heard people saying downtown they believe he's here."

Nero snorted. "Hardly. We'd have been able to sense a ghost too."

Nero looked at the dirt a few seconds more before

joining Marlowe in the sun. Something was definitely odd about this whole business. Maybe a nap would help. He'd seen Josie at the town common earlier in the day and had a funny feeling she might be heading down the wrong path. He needed to reroute her by showing her clues that would lead to the real killer... Too bad he had no idea who that was.

*

After my visit with Jen, I hurried back to the guesthouse. If Flora hadn't cleaned Millie's great-grandmother's doily, I wanted to be sure I got it done right away. I should clean all the doilies really. They'd been here for a couple hundred years and I didn't want one to be cleaner than the others. How did you clean a doily anyway? Could you put it in the washing machine with bleach? Maybe I should ask Flora. No. She didn't seem to know a lot about cleaning. Hand washing was probably best.

I stepped into the foyer, surprised to see Nero and Marlowe on the table, sniffing around the doily. They turned as I came in and I could have sworn their looks were a tad judgmental. Were they the cleaning police now, judging me for not getting the doily cleaned right away?

"I know, I know. It's dirty." I shooed them away to find that the doily was not dirty at all, apart from a few little pieces of dirt that the cats had apparently decided were quite fascinating. Flora must've cleaned the doily, but left loose dirt. No surprise there. I could at least give her credit for the effort, and Millie's family doily wasn't ruined.

Meow.

Nero blinked at me with his intelligent golden eyes as if he was trying to tell me something.

"Yes, I already admitted that I see there's dirt here." I brushed the dirt into my palm, making a mental note to wash off the table later.

Mewp.

Marlowe jumped down and sniffed my shoes.

"My shoes aren't dirty. I'm not the one who was out digging for treasure," I said.

Both cats blinked up at me, their tails swishing. The intensity of their stares gave me the impression that they were either trying to telepath some thoughts my way or were thinking I was the dumbest human around. Maybe both. Then again, maybe they just wanted some food.

"Are you guys hungry?" I'd been making attempts to communicate with them as equals. I'd really been trying to see if they had any understanding of my questions. I still wasn't convinced that they were as smart as Millie seemed to think, but at times they did seem eerily intelligent.

Meroo!

They both ran to the kitchen. Just as I thought, my attempts at communication were getting better.

Flora walked in the front door just then, wearing a crocheted sweater with the sleeves rolled up to her elbows and her giant beige patent-leather purse hanging from her arm.

"Oh, Flora, there you are."

She scowled at me. "Where else would I be?"

"Where have you been?"

Flora sighed and rolled her eyes, the thick round coke-bottle glasses giving this a comical effect. "I told you earlier. I was going to Irma Blazer's to work on our cookies for the great-grandmothers of twins' table." She spoke slowly as if I was a dunce and couldn't understand her. "I left shortly after Seth Chamberlain interrogated me."

Now I remembered. Flora had mentioned that the other day, but with all the excitement going on, I'd forgotten.

"Oh, right. How did that go with Seth anyway?" I asked.

Flora pursed her lips as she put her giant purse down on the table, shrugged out of her sweater and hung it on the coatrack. "That young man needs to learn some manners. Accusing his elders. I don't know what the world is coming to."

I bit back a smile. Seth had to be almost seventy and I didn't think he was that much younger than Flora. Then again, she said she changed his diapers, so there must have been at least a decade and a few years between them.

"I don't know what gives him cause to accuse you. You weren't even out there digging, right?" Flora had been cagey about this before and I wanted to ask again because Flora was getting up there in years and maybe she was having some memory issues. Paula had claimed to have seen her. Myron had said Flora got the last shovel. Paula couldn't actually be trusted to remember stuff right and Myron could have been lying, but why would he?

Flora pressed her lips together and fisted her hands on her hips. "I never said I wasn't out there. I said I couldn't very well clobber someone over the head. I don't have the strength." She bent her scrawny arm at the elbow again to make a muscle, as if to prove her point. "But just like everyone else in town I was curious about the treasure, so I wanted to see what was going on."

I searched my memory banks for the previous conversation. Flora was right, she had said she couldn't clobber someone. But I still got the impression she'd purposely avoided admitting she was out there. Maybe she was embarrassed about digging. Or afraid about being accused? But she hadn't actually lied, I'd just misinterpreted what she'd said. That made me feel a lot better. "So you *were* digging?"

Flora looked appropriately embarrassed. "As much as I could. It's hard work."

That explained why Paula had seen her. But it didn't explain something else I'd heard about her.

"Are you planning on going on a trip?" I asked.

Flora frowned at me. "No. What makes you ask that? Where would I get money for a trip?"

"Oh, I don't know. I thought I heard from someone that you were taking one." I didn't want to rat out Annabel. No sense in making enemies out of someone you might want to get information from later.

Flora's gigantic eyes assessed me as if she was considering having me committed. Butterflies swarmed in my gut. Either Annabel had gotten her wires crossed or Flora was a very good actress. And if it was the latter,

then all the details of her being capable of hitting someone with a shovel could have been acting too.

"I would have asked for the time off if I was going on
a trip, right? Did I ask for time off?" Flora reached into
the closet and pulled out the feather duster.

"No. But if you want some time off you can have it."

"Got no need for time off. Got no need for travel.
Now, if you don't mind, I have to get cleaning. Lots
of work to do." She shuffled off toward the stairs then
stopped, turning to look at me. "By the way, don't
worry. I did clean that room for that nasty Arlene. You
ask me, she doesn't deserve it. The place was a pigsty.
But that's none of my business."

"Thanks. And thanks for cleaning off the doily too."
I gestured toward the table. I didn't mention she'd forgotten to pick up some of the dirt. With Flora you had
to take what you get.

She gave me another one of those I-should-have-
you-committed looks. "If you say so."

Merup.

The cats had been sitting patiently watching us as if
they understood every word we were saying. But now it
appeared their patience had come to an end. They trotted toward the kitchen, glancing back at me every few
steps. They wanted the food I'd promised earlier.

Flora was swatting at the railing with the duster as
she ascended the stairs. I was glad she hadn't lied about
being out there last night. Paula probably had seen her
but been confused about where and when. Okay, the
thing about the trip was a little odd but maybe Flora
didn't want me to know she was planning one or

maybe she was looking into it for one of her bazillion grandchildren.

I could cross Flora off my suspect list and focus on the others. The Biddeford siblings were at the top and I couldn't discount Doris, either. Myron was running a close second, though. He'd lied about being here, but I felt that might be because he was embarrassed to admit he was with Stella. Too bad we didn't know more about the arguments among the Biddeford clan. So far it didn't seem like any of them were worth killing over. I needed someone with a more compelling motive.

At least the townspeople wouldn't be digging up the yard again. If what Jen said was true, they were all too afraid of Jedediah Biddeford's ghost. But I didn't think Bob's death had been perpetrated by any ghost. No, whoever clobbered Bob over the head was undoubtedly human, and might be getting very nervous about being discovered as the killer.

And, as I knew from previous experience, people who were nervous about being exposed as a killer could become very dangerous.

Chapter Seventeen

I shook off the silly notion that Jedediah's ghost was killing people who had been searching for his treasure and fed the cats. They seemed to appreciate their meal of turkey chunks and gravy if the way they circled around my feet and rubbed their cheeks on my ankles was any indication.

I bent down to pet them, and they rewarded me by butting their soft heads against my hand and purring. My relationship with the cats was improving greatly. I'd never had a cat before buying the guesthouse and I had to admit they were actually quite good pets.

"You know, you guys are actually pretty great. I'm glad to own you."

The cats abruptly stopped their purring and rubbing, and looked at me with eyes that were practically shooting daggers.

"I mean, I'm glad you guys own me now."

That must have mollified them because they continued their purring and rubbing—it was as if they could understand every word I'd said.

The cats went back to their bowls and I stood and watched them eat for a few seconds. Unlike humans, the cats seemed to appreciate most things I gave them, except when they were being finicky. Turns out cats are pretty good company too. Maybe even better company than husbands. I certainly enjoyed my relationship with them more than the last several years—possibly even the last several decades—with my ex, Clive.

I left the cats to their bowls and pulled out Millie's recipe file. I needed to find something for breakfast the next day. The Oyster Cove Guesthouse didn't provide lunch or dinner, but the guests sure did expect a spectacular breakfast.

I riffled through the file, discarding the ones that seemed like they were beyond my skill set or that had too many ingredients, when the back door opened and in came my mother and Millie.

"I hope you don't mind us just walking in, dear." Millie came over to inspect the recipes I'd pulled out. "Are you planning for breakfast tomorrow? That's very good. You need to plan ahead when you are running an operation like this. What are you going to make?"

The cats immediately ran over to greet Millie but I noticed this time they hesitated just for a second, looking up as if to assure me that even though they were meeting their old friend Millie, they still knew that their new friend—me—was the one who fed them. I found that heartwarming even if it was likely just my imagination.

"I'm not sure. I was thinking about maybe a quiche or a frittata, but I've never made a frittata..." I glanced at Millie hopefully. So far Millie had helped me cook most of the breakfasts I'd served. I guess she felt a responsibility to keep up the reputation of the guesthouse in that department. I didn't mind.

"We have a lot going on, so I think a quiche would do. You know you can make those ahead of time." Millie selected a broccoli quiche recipe and put it on the counter. "You have some leftover cooked white rice from our Chinese takeout the other day, don't you?"

"Yep."

"Perfect. I don't like to waste food. We can use that up in here," Millie said. "You know, back when I ran the guesthouse in my younger days, I used to like to pre-prep. Some things like the frittata must be prepared fresh that morning, but I always preferred doing something the night before, that way I didn't have to get up early. I could just rush down, heat it up and then put it on the breakfast buffet with the other items. I never did like to get up early."

"All those late nights out with your boyfriends," my mother teased.

Millie blushed and fluffed her hair. "Well now, I guess I'll just start assembling these ingredients."

She opened the cupboard and took out some salt and pepper, then grabbed eggs, cheese and milk and the rice out of the fridge before taking the frozen broccoli out of the freezer and popping it into the microwave. "It's always a good idea to have some frozen veggies around, comes in handy when you need to whip up a quiche."

I nodded. The broccoli must have been left over from when Millie owned the place. I certainly didn't remember buying it.

As she worked, she talked. "Did you learn anything new about…" She jerked her head in the direction of the pond.

"I talked to Jen and she said people around town think Jedediah's ghost came back and committed the murder."

My mother gave a nervous laugh, her eyes darting around the room as if she expected a ghost to manifest out of nowhere. "That's ridiculous. Isn't it?"

"Yes, of course it is." Millie cracked an egg into a bowl and started beating it. "That man was definitely killed by a human. He was bludgeoned over the head with a shovel. Ghosts would do something less physical."

"I think all of Bob's siblings are still suspects. I'm not sure about Flora, she did say she was out there... but she didn't kill Bob, of course." I chewed on my bottom lip. Should I mention to Mom and Millie that she'd sort of lied? Millie would probably say she had just been forgetful, she *was* quite old. I wondered if the police still suspected her.

"I haven't talked to Seth Chamberlain, have you?" I asked. Millie always could wrangle sensitive information out of him.

Millie blushed. Just as I suspected, she'd been doing more than talking with Sheriff Chamberlain. Good thing for us, though, as we could use all the information we could get.

Millie added rice to the egg and beat faster. "I happen to know the siblings are still suspects but don't tell anyone I told you."

"All of them?" my mother asked as Marlowe jumped up onto her lap. "I thought maybe Earl had cleared himself with the shoes."

Millie nodded. "Yes. His Nikes do seem to clear him, but who can believe what Paula said? Maybe she didn't see fancy shoes at all."

"And is she a suspect?" I asked. "I mean, she does admit she was in proximity. She *says* she was asleep under the bench, but she could be lying about that."

"I don't think we can rule any of them out because they all argued with Bob," Mom said.

"And Flora didn't," Millie added. "She has no motive."

"Other than the treasure," Mom added.

"If only we knew what those arguments were really about we could determine if his siblings had something to kill over," I said.

"And let's not forget about Myron Remington. He was acting very strange and overly interested in the case. He dresses fancy. I bet he has a pair of Italian leather shoes like Paula said she saw. Didn't you see him here last night, Millie?" my mother asked.

"Yep. I think he was with Stella Dumont, but you're wrong about one thing. He's not really interested in Bob's case, he's more interested in Jedediah's case. The skeleton," Millie said. "He was asking Seth all about it."

Millie had mixed grated cheese in with the egg and rice and she pressed that into a pie plate to make the crust. I watched carefully. Millie made it look easy.

"Myron said he wasn't here that night," I said. Millie turned to look at me, her left brow quirked up. "I asked him directly."

"I saw him. I know it was him," Millie said.

"Why would he lie?" my mother asked.

"If he was with Stella he might not want anyone to know," I suggested.

"Or maybe he's the killer and pretending he is interested in the skeleton as an excuse to find out more about the police investigation into Bob's murder," Mom said.

Millie mixed the rest of the eggs and the other ingredients together and poured it in the pie plate on top of the egg and rice crust. The cats begged and she tossed them a piece of cheese. "I don't know. Myron has always been worried about what people think. Always boasting about how his family has been here for generations, as if that was some sort of pedigree. He probably just didn't want anyone to know that he'd lowered himself to the level of regular folks."

"Did Flora say what she was doing down by the pond? Or even if she *was* there?" Mom asked.

"Not to me," I said. "I didn't hear her deny Paula's accusation either, though."

Millie pressed her lips together. "Seth didn't mention what he talked about with Flora. I know he thinks I am biased about her. But if Paula is telling the truth and she was awakened by the shoe stepping on her hand, *then* saw Flora, that means Flora was coming down the path after the person with the fancy shoes," Millie said. "Do you think Flora might've seen something and is afraid to talk about it?"

The cats meowed loudly. They were over by a small bookshelf that held ephemera related to the guesthouse. All kinds of old brochures, menus, pictures. Nero swatted at the little blue plastic ring from a milk bottle that had fallen on the floor and it skittered under the bookshelf. The two cats peered after it, then Marlowe snaked her paw under to retrieve it.

"She might have seen something, but I doubt it," Millie said. "I mean, have you ever seen Flora afraid to speak up?"

"Good point," I said. "And what about this business about a trip to the Caribbean? Why would Annabel say Flora was taking one if she isn't? Or if she is, why would Flora lie?"

Millie waved her hands dismissively. "Annabel probably thinks if she says it enough times Flora will think it's her idea. She's doing a big renovation on her travel agency and I bet she needs the money. I wouldn't be surprised if she's saying that about everyone—you know, planting the idea sort of like a subliminal message."

"Maybe. I just hope Seth will leave Flora alone now. He has many more interesting suspects to consider," I said.

"Not the least of which is Jedediah's ghost." Mom stared at the cats, who were now staring at the bookcase as if mesmerized by something the rest of us couldn't see. "Maybe Nero and Marlowe know more about that than we do."

Mew!

They turned to look at us as if they knew we were talking about them, then continued playing with the plastic ring, Nero swatting at it and sending it skidding into the butler's pantry.

"Oh, go on." Millie waved her hand in the air. "You don't believe that, do you?"

"Maybe not, but plenty of people *do* believe it."

Mom glanced at me. "I just hope it doesn't hurt the reputation of the guesthouse."

"All the more reason to figure out who really killed Bob so the rumors can stop." I would like nothing better than to solve this case quickly and move on. I hadn't gotten a reservation for the guesthouse in the last couple of days and soon the Biddefords would be leaving. I needed new guests to pay the bills. And I didn't need something like a lingering murder investigation to scare them off.

Millie shoved the quiche into the oven. "I'm just going to cook this for a while to let it set and you can heat it up tomorrow morning. Now, let's talk about the town celebration. Are you all set with the rest of the display items and the loaf cakes?"

"Sure." I was a bit reluctant to stop the murder discussion since I really wanted to figure out who the killer was, but I supposed that talking about something else would give our collective subconscious time to work on all the clues and suspects. "I'll dig up that book on the guesthouse history from my room tonight. I made a trial batch of apple-pecan loaf." I gestured toward the loaf I'd left cooling.

"I saw that. Was wondering when you were going to let me try it." Millie cut into the loaf and I held my breath as she took a bite and swirled it around in her mouth like she was taste-testing fine wine.

"It's okay. A little tart." Millie picked up the recipe card and looked over the recipe. "Oh yes, I remember this one. You might want to add a pinch more sugar. Plenty of people like it sweet. And you have the little mini loaf pans and bows?"

"Yep." I can't tell you how relieved I was the loaf had passed Millie's taste test. Sure, she'd complained about it being tart, but the fact that that was all she'd had to say was a high compliment. Millie had given me these cute miniature tinfoil loaf pans, pink plastic wrap and red bows. She'd said the presentation would draw people to my table. I was afraid I needed as much help as I could to get people in my line and out of Stella's, so I was willing to try anything, even if it meant pouring batter into dozens of tiny pans.

"Okay." Millie brought her hands together and looked at my mother. "What do you say we leave Josie to it? The bingo game at the senior center starts in thirty minutes and it's a double pot tonight. Don't want to miss it."

"You guys take off, I can handle this." I gestured toward the oven.

"Great." Millie pointed. "Let that cook for twenty more minutes, then let it cool and put it in the fridge. Heat it up tomorrow morning for about fifteen or twenty minutes. Easy peasy."

The cats trotted out to say their goodbyes and Millie and Mom went out the back door. As I was watching them go, Millie turned and said, "Don't worry, Josie, everything will work out perfectly. You'll see."

"That's right," Mom agreed. "But you might want to burn some sage, just in case those rumors about Jedediah's ghost really are true."

*

No sooner had Mom and Millie left than the front door opened and I heard the Biddefords come in. At least they wouldn't be digging up the yard tonight. The police had taken their shovels, but I also doubted they would be so cold-hearted to want to dig when that's how their brother had been killed. I lurked in the hallway, hidden by the staircase—not to eavesdrop, but to give them some privacy. Okay, maybe I wanted to eavesdrop a little. They were my prime suspects and one of them might say something incriminating.

"I think a nice simple service with no wake is fine," Carla said. "We don't really need to rub elbows with any of Bob's unsavory acquaintances, so there's no need for a wake."

"If the police ever release the body," Earl said.

"Maybe someone could do a cheese sculpture of a dove to put on top of the casket?" Doris asked.

The kids mumbled their agreement.

"White cheddar would work well for that," Paula said.

"Boy, that Marinara Mariner sure has spicy sauce. I'll be up all night." Earl burped.

"Maybe you shouldn't have eaten so much," Carla said. I could hear her sniffing. "Did Josie bake something? Maybe we should make sure the kitchen isn't on fire."

The siblings laughed and I resisted the urge to march right out there and give them a piece of my mind. I'd burned a few loaf cakes since the Biddefords had been here, but I didn't burn *everything* I put in the oven.

"I'm going to bed to see if I can get some sleep," Arlene said. "It's kind of freaky knowing there is a murderer running around. I knew this town was weird.

Luckily, we'll only be here a few more days. I don't even care about the town celebration or how Earl's ancestors practically founded Oyster Cove anymore."

"You can say that again," Carla agreed. "And honestly, I don't know if I want to sleep in this creepy old house with Jedediah Biddeford's ghost rambling around. I don't want to be his next victim."

"You don't really think there is a ghost here, do you?" Arlene scoffed.

"That's what they're saying in town."

Great. People were starting to believe this murdering ghost nonsense. Now even the current guests were afraid to stay. I heard the stairs creaking as they all went up to bed.

"You know, it would make sense that it would be Jed's ghost," Earl said. "I mean, who else would want to kill Bob?"

"You mean other than one of *ush*?" Paula slurred.

"Yeah," Earl said. "Maybe Bob really did find something and Jed made good on his curse to harm whoever messed with his treasure."

"Stop it!" Arlene admonished. "I won't sleep a wink. There's no such thing as ghosts."

"Well, I, for one, hope there really is," Doris said. "And I hope Jed is rambling around in here. In fact, I hope he pays me a visit tonight."

"Why is that?" Henry asked.

"Because then maybe I can persuade him to tell me where he hid the darn treasure!"

Chapter Eighteen

The cats had been sitting silently at my feet the whole time I listened to the Biddefords' conversation. They blinked up at me as if in agreement that the whole family was crazy. But was one of them a killer?

Nero rubbed his face on my ankle and then looked up at me adoringly. I could see why people got so attached to the furry creatures. I was really starting to like them; they could be very friendly and attentive. They were especially attentive when I headed toward the fridge and got out some cheese and an apple for a snack.

"You guys want a snack too? Okay, maybe a little cheese." I broke off two pieces and added it to my plate. At their protesting meows I articulated, "You can have these up in our room after I get this quiche out of the oven."

Our room. Who knew I'd be thinking of the cats as part of my family in that way?

Meow! they chorused.

Sounded like they'd understood. But when I started toward the back stairs, after securing the quiche in the fridge, the cats meowed loudly . . . prancing off in the direction of the butler's pantry. Did they not understand we were going to our room? Or maybe I was the one who didn't understand. I decided to follow them and find out.

As I started toward them Nero's tail twitched and he trotted off even further, casting glances over his shoulder as if to make sure I was following. I'd determined he was the smarter of the two after watching them interact. Marlowe seemed younger, more impetuous. Marlowe had trotted ahead not even looking back, her tail waving in the air like a flag to follow.

The other side of the pantry opened into the hallway. At first, I thought they'd go toward the west wing. That seemed to be where everything happened. Bodies, skeletons, who knew what would be next? To my relief, they veered off to the right continuing down the hall to the conservatory.

Oh, no. Was something wrong in there now? Had Ed started work and uncovered something dastardly or, even worse, been injured? I'd given Ed the day off but it would be just like him to come in and work anyway. The room was off the beaten path and no one would be walking past it to look in and see if someone was hurt in there.

We came to the French doors that opened into the room and my fears were put to rest when I saw it was empty except for the plants Millie had given me. Maybe the cats were trying to remind me to water them.

"Nice try, guys. Everything looks fine in here." I scanned the room. Even in its dilapidated state, it was clearly once lovely. Large Palladian windows—most of which were temporarily boarded up—ran the length of the room and French doors opened to the overgrown garden. The moon shone in from the one window not boarded, creating a swatch of silver light on the floor. Wait…what was that shadow on the floor, over by the giant ficus tree?

The cats trotted over. Uh oh…was this why they'd come here? Dread washed over me. The cats always seemed to insist on summoning humans when something terrible had happened.

The electricity had been shut off to this room, so I ventured in to get a closer look. I bent down slowly… phew! It was only dirt.

"Hey, did you guys do this?" I asked.

The cats looked up at me, the moonlight reflected in their eyes, making them glow bright. I inspected the ficus. Yep, looked like someone had rummaged in the dirt. I was pretty sure the cats liked to dig. I'd seen them digging outside.

"It's not nice to dig in the house. That's for outside."

They gave off some confused meows. Nero batted at the dirt.

"Don't spread it around or you won't get any treats." I tapped the plate with the cheese.

Mew!

Marlowe had something in the corner. I hoped it wasn't a mouse. She crouched down and swatted. It rolled out toward me. Thankfully too small to be a mouse. I bent down to pick it up. A shiny nail? Had Ed been working in here? He'd said he hadn't started here yet.

I stood and looked around. I didn't see any tools or any evidence that work had been done. The nail could have come from anywhere, though; the cats were known for batting things around and then leaving them in other rooms. They particularly liked the plastic water bottle caps. They must have batted the nail in here all the way from the ballroom.

They were looking up at me as if expecting praise. I held the nail out to them. "I don't think it's a good idea to be batting nails all over the house. A guest could step on one and become injured."

The cats looked at each other, shook their heads and trotted off. I looked back at the dirt as I left. Too bad I couldn't train them to pick it up. I'd have to have Flora do it. Maybe it wasn't a good idea to have plants in the house with the cats? And they must not be as smart as I'd been giving them credit for if they led me to their mess.

I followed them to the owner's quarters, a cozy suite with a window overlooking the ocean. It was in a rounded turret and had a cute sitting area in the round part. The neutral shades of mocha and heather were soothing. I loved retreating here at the end of the day.

Millie had left quite a few of the antiques that decorated the room, but it also had some modern touches like a comfy micro-suede sectional. I settled onto the couch and the cats jumped up beside me, looking expectantly from me to the cheese.

"I did promise you some, didn't I?" I took the two small pieces and broke them up some more, then held one out to Nero, who sniffed it for what seemed like an hour before gently taking it.

"And you?" I held one out to Marlowe. She glanced

at Nero who was still busy daintily eating, then sniffed twice and grabbed it.

I nibbled my piece and thought about the day. I was a bit disturbed by the conversation I'd overheard in the hallway. I certainly hoped people weren't going to start spreading rumors about a murderous ghost. All the more reason to find the killer pronto.

But the murder investigation wasn't the only thing I had on my plate. I had to juggle that along with my responsibilities for the town celebration. I had the ingredients for the loaf cake I planned to make all ready to go and I'd do another test run tomorrow morning. The pamphlets were already on the table. I just needed that book about the Oyster Cove Guesthouse history. Millie said that should be up here, so I put my snack down and went over to the antique oak bookcase in the turret part of the room.

Meow!

Nero hopped on top of the bookshelf and peered down at me.

"Where's the book, buddy?" I waited for him to indicate the general location but all he did was stare at me.

"Okay..." I ran my fingers along the leather-bound spines of the books. Poetry. *Uncle Tom's Cabin*. An Audubon anthology. My fingers stopped at a large book. "*Oyster Cove Town History*. This must be it."

Merooo... Marlowe stared at me from the back of the couch.

"Right, I thought so." I took the book and flopped down on the couch. Nero trotted over. Both he and Marlowe seemed overly interested in the book, sniffing at it and putting their paws on it.

"You want to see what's inside? I do too." I opened the book, inhaling the vanilla scent of age-old paper. Inside were pictures of the guesthouse back in Jed's day. It had been a large house but not nearly as large as it was now. Jed stood in front alongside a woman in a black dress with a voluminous skirt.

I pointed the woman out. "I guess this is Mrs. Jed."

Nero smacked his paw on the page right above the description. Yep, Helena Biddeford. It was his wife.

"Maybe she's the one who put him in the wall. What do you guys think?"

Meroo.

Marlowe pushed the edge of the book and it flipped to the next page.

"Going too slow for you?"

I flipped through, marveling at the old photos of the guesthouse and the town. Things had changed a lot over the centuries. There was a picture of a realistic drawing of Jedediah Biddeford with his family and household staff. He had his hand on a cane, the ring found on the skeleton clearly evident on his finger.

"I wonder which one of these children is Doris's ancestor?" Doris hadn't mentioned the name of the ancestor at the top of the Biddeford tree, but I looked at the inscription under the image anyway.

A familiar name caught my eye. Thomas Remington. Was that Myron's ancestor?

I pulled the book closer to my face. He kind of looked like Myron. But this guy wasn't a wealthy banker, he was a servant.

"Looks like Myron's ancestor was Jedediah Biddeford's butler," I said out loud to the cats, who both were staring at me. "Funny how things work out, huh? He's always boasting how his family was one of the first in Oyster Cove, but he makes it sound like they were part of the upper class."

Meroo. Nero's paw shot out and he riffled the pages, losing my place in the book.

"Yeah, I agree Myron sure is uppity considering where he came from." I flipped back to the page just to double-check.

Meyawl! Marlowe whacked the cover of the book and I caught the pages before it snapped shut.

"Hey, I can't read if—" Wait. Was their behavior an indication that I was on to something? They did have an uncanny way of knowing what was going on and it had seemed like they had helped me out during the last investigation, though I didn't want to admit it at the time. Now that I'd spent more time with them, I was more inclined to consider that they might be smarter than everyone thought.

I broke off two more small pieces of cheese as a reward. I didn't want to give them too much lest it upset their delicate systems. "I think you guys are trying to tell me something, aren't you? Is this why Myron lied about being here last night? Does he have something to do with this?"

Meroo.

Merow.

The cats looked at me funny as if they didn't understand what the reward was about, but they weren't about to pass up cheese because they gobbled it down before head-butting my hand and practically shutting the book in their zeal to be petted.

Shutting the book wasn't a bad idea. I didn't need to read further. I was pretty sure I was on to something. Myron's ancestor was the butler to Jedediah, and butlers always knew all their masters' secrets. What if one of those secrets was the location of the treasure? And what if that location got passed down through the generations?

But if it had, wouldn't someone have dug it up by now? Why would Myron wait so long and why was he over by the gazebo, which would be the least likely place for Jedediah to have buried it? Not to mention that Bob had been killed at the pond, which was very far from the gazebo. What if it was Myron who found the treasure and Bob who caught him and tried to take it? And did that mean there really was treasure after all?

Some of this didn't add up, but one thing was fishy. Myron had lied about being here and if that didn't indicate guilt about something, I didn't know what did!

I might have to do some digging, but I knew one thing for sure—I was finally starting to understand what the cats were trying to tell me!

Chapter Nineteen

"Josie still does not quite understand what we are trying to tell her," Marlowe said from her perch near the pantry the next morning as they watched Josie heat up the quiche in the oven.

"But at least she is open to the fact that we are trying to tell her *something*. She needs more work, but this is a start," said Nero.

"Start schmart, she needs to listen to us now or she's going to end up in trouble just like she did with the last murder." Marlowe eyed the countertop where the dishes were drying. "We may need to do something drastic."

Nero sighed. "I know. Unfortunately, she is going down the wrong path. She totally misinterpreted our hints about that history book. There are much more interesting suspects to pursue than Myron Remington."

"True. Though it is interesting that his family was connected with the Biddefords. I thought I smelled something familiar on him too," Marlowe said.

Nero glanced at the tortie as she strutted over to the countertop. Had Marlowe really developed such a keen sense of smell or was she just saying that to make herself seem smart? It was true Myron had smelled familiar, but it wasn't because some ancestor had once worked in the house. No, Nero suspected there was an entirely different reason and he needed to clue Josie in on it.

"What are you kitties up to?" Josie stood hands on hips watching them. "Do you need a treat for all your good work last night?"

Nero gave her his most adorable head tilt.

Meow.

Josie opened the fridge and Marlowe hopped up onto the countertop and started batting at the dishes. Josie backed out of the fridge with a plate in her hand then scowled at Marlowe. "No, don't do that. Especially not that Yale mug. Carla will have a fit."

Josie picked Marlowe up and placed her on the floor then put down a small dish with some little bite-sized tidbits of steak inside.

"That's very good steak, so you guys chew slowly and savor it."

Marlowe eagerly got to work on the steak along with Nero.

"We're going to have to push her in the right direction, somehow," Nero said between mouthfuls. "We need to show her that Myron is not up to what she thinks he is."

"But we don't know for sure, do we?" Marlowe asked. "He *could* be the killer."

"Perhaps. He could be involved, but remember that Juliette heard a woman in the confessional." Nero finished off the last of the steak just as Ed O'Hara appeared in the doorway.

Nero knew the elderly gentleman had something of a crush on Josie, though their ages were mismatched.

The smile on Ed's face as he silently watched Josie work left little doubt. It was all harmless. Ed's wife had passed a few years prior and he needed something to focus on. He would never actually try to ask Josie for a date. Besides, Josie was perfect for Millie's nephew Mike. Everyone but Josie could see that.

"I could get to work on the ballroom again today, Ms. Waters," Ed said.

Josie jerked and turned to look at him. "Oh, Ed! You scared me."

"I snuck up on you like a ghost." Ed smiled, the weathered lines around his eyes crinkling.

"Yeah, like Jedediah's ghost."

"I hope you're not scared because of those rumors, they don't mean nothing."

"Well, I certainly know that," Josie said. "Even if half the town thinks a ghost killed Bob Biddeford."

"Yeah."

"Hey, Ed, if you got any work done in the conservatory, did you happen to tip over a plant?"

"No. I never got set up in there because you gave me the day off, then this morning I heard the ballroom had been cleared by the cops." Ed's gaze drifted to Nero and Marlowe. "Must've been those cats, because I certainly would have no reason to be in there."

Josie frowned at them and Nero's spirits sank. Though he wasn't beholden to having the human like him, he still felt the need to be accepted by her. Though he considered Millie to be his real human, Josie was the one he had now, and her disapproval cut deeply. Besides, they weren't the ones who made the mess. At least, not that time. Just another example of Josie misinterpreting their communications. He looked at Ed suspiciously; he was certain the old man had been in the conservatory, but why would he lie to Josie about it? He made a mental note to keep a close eye on Ed. But right now he had more important things to do.

"Bad kitties. I expect you not to do that anymore."

Marlowe swished her tail and looked at Nero. "How do you like that? She thinks we made that mess."

"Yeah. Well, if she doesn't know what's good for her, we're gonna have to show her what's good for her."

Nero took the opportunity to hop up on the counter while Josie was distracted by talking to Ed. He pushed gently at the dishes. He didn't want to push too hard lest they fall off onto the floor and smash. Some of them were dishes that Millie had collected for the guesthouse and he couldn't bear to see them in pieces on the floor. Somehow, he needed to get Josie thinking along the right lines.

"I've just taken a quiche out of the oven." Josie gestured toward the steaming pie plate on the counter. "I was about to cut pieces for the serving tray if you'd like one."

"Don't mind if I do." Ed came into the kitchen and Josie turned her back, not even watching Nero's attempts at communication.

"She's not even watching us," Marlowe said, disgusted.

"Are those cats supposed to be on the counter?" Ed asked.

Josie turned around, pressing her lips together when she saw Nero at the dishes. "No. And luckily our building inspector is a little bit nicer than the last one and probably wouldn't rat me out, but still I don't relish being closed down by the Board of Health."

She marched over to the counter and picked up Nero—not very gently, either—and plopped him down on the floor. "Now you stay down there. I don't want to have to banish you guys from the kitchen."

Josie went back to cutting up the quiche while Nero and Marlowe rolled their eyes at each other.

"Doesn't Josie know that cats don't do as they're told?" Marlowe asked.

"No kidding. Human orders rankle us and we tend to do the exact opposite."

"Yeah, and in this case it's for her own good. Maybe once she's not distracted with Ed she'll understand what we're trying to say. But we may have to take more drastic action."

"I'll get her to understand." Nero hopped up on the counter again. He pushed the Yale mug so that the edge of it hung precariously over the lip of the countertop.

Ed looked up from the slice of the quiche Josie had put on a dainty floral plate in front of him. "Hey! That cat's gonna knock that mug to the floor."

Josie whirled around, her eyes zoning in on the blue Yale mug. Her hand shot out and snatched it from harm's way.

"Bad kitty. Now if you broke that Carla would be—" And then Josie's eyes widened. She glanced at the mug, then back at Nero. Their eyes locked and in that instant Nero knew Josie had finally gotten the message he was trying to send.

"Finally," Marlowe said as she jumped onto the counter to join him.

Movement outside the window caught Nero's eye.

"Isn't that Harry and Stubbs out there in the shrubs?" Marlowe asked.

Nero craned his neck to see further. The tortie was right. The two cats were pacing back and forth and looking over at the guesthouse. "It is them...It looks like they've found something important."

*

I stared at the Yale coffee mug in my hand. Myron had gone to a fancy college, had it been Yale? Is that why Myron had been at the gazebo when Bob was killed at the pond? He was working with someone else. Carla. Hadn't Doris said that Carla wasn't very bright because she'd been lurking around near the gazebo?

Maybe that's why Stella had said something about Myron not deserving treasure. Maybe she had her sights set on Myron and saw him with Carla. Had Bob known about Carla and Myron and threatened to tell on her? But would that really be worth killing him over? Maybe it would if treasure was involved.

Myron and Carla were around the same age. If Myron had also attended Yale, it was possible they knew each other, but I had to find out for sure.

But first, I had to get this apple-pecan bread in the oven.

I sliced off another piece of quiche for Ed and sent him off to the west wing, then chopped the pecans and apples and mixed eggs, oil and vanilla, setting everything aside while I mixed together the flour, baking soda and cinnamon. I combined the wet ingredients with the dry into a thick batter and poured some into one of the tiny loaf pans and shoved it in the oven, then set the timer for ninety minutes after double-checking the directions for cooking time on Millie's recipe. I wasn't going to let it burn again!

I quickly got the breakfast trays together. The guests would be down in ten minutes but usually I could find Doris wandering around downstairs. If I could get her aside privately I might be able to find out when Carla went to Yale. I knew that Myron had gone after we graduated high school, so if Carla attended in the late 1980s it was possible they knew each other. I didn't want Carla to overhear the question, though, so I had to catch Doris before Carla came down.

I rushed over to the parlor. No sign of Doris. Maybe she was in the back sitting room? Nope. The conservatory? Nada. Darn. I was coming back down the hall when I saw Earl staring at the door to the west wing. It was open, likely because Ed was moving tools in. I could hear Ed inside setting things up.

"Can I help you?" I asked Earl.

He turned around, his face white as a sheet. "Look, Jedediah's ghost has left the door open! He's coming for the rest of us!"

"Hardly," Ed's voice came from inside. "I'm just coming back to shut it. Had my hands full with my tools."

"That's just the carpenter, Ed. Besides, why would Jedediah be coming back to kill you? Nobody got the treasure, right? And the curse was that he was gonna do away with anyone who had his treasure." I steered Earl away from the door as Ed shut it from the other side.

Ed was supposed to keep the door shut so that guests didn't wander onto the worksite, and he was very good about it. I glanced down. There was no gap between the bottom of the door and the floor. If the cats had batted a nail from this wing into the conservatory, I was sure they would have had to bat it under this door. The other exits were too far away. But there was no gap to push it through, so if the cats hadn't moved the nail, then how did it get into the conservatory? Had Ed lied about being in there? Maybe I needed to expand my suspect list to include Ed, but right now I had to focus on finding out about Carla and Myron.

Earl frowned. "Yeah, but somebody killed Bob."

"Are you sure that had something to do with the treasure?"

Earl's eyes narrowed. "I thought so. This place might not be safe with a murdering ghost around."

I fought the urge to roll my eyes. Not only was the notion of a murdering ghost absurd, I sure as heck didn't need him spreading that rumor around town.

"I'm sure the police will find out that whoever killed Bob was no ghost." Or, more likely, my mother, Millie and I would.

Earl didn't look convinced. He glanced down at the mug in my hand. "Is that Carla's mug?"

I'd almost forgotten I was carrying it. "Yeah. I washed it out and was returning it to the dining room so she could have it for her morning coffee."

"Thought so. She acts like that thing is the Holy Grail, for crying out loud, brings it everywhere. It's kind of embarrassing. You should see her at the office. She has a fit if anyone touches it."

Maybe it wasn't so bad that I'd encountered Earl in the hallway. He'd probably know what years Carla went to Yale. And the conversation about the mug was the perfect opportunity to ask. Not to mention no one else was in the hallway to hear us.

"I guess it's quite an accomplishment to graduate from Yale, though, right?"

Earl shrugged. "I guess. I went to Stanford."

I nodded. "That's a good school too. Are you older than Carla? Were you guys in college the same time?"

"I'm a few years older. Graduated in 1987."

I did the math. Myron and Carla would have been at Yale at the same time. It was possible they'd worked together to kill Bob...but why?

"Is breakfast ready?" Earl asked, startling me out of my reverie.

"Almost. Go ahead in there and I will get everything set up for you."

I rushed back into the kitchen after putting the mug on the sideboard where Carla liked it to be placed right next to the coffee urn, which I noticed with approval Flora had already set to percolating.

I rushed back into the kitchen, gathered the breakfast items together and walked them out to the sideboard.

I hovered in the doorway, watching everyone eat contentedly, if not a bit solemnly. They were shoveling in the quiche. No one complained about the lack of pancakes. *Had one of them killed Bob?*

My eyes drifted to the Yale mug. That mug could be the key to uncovering what really happened. But I still wondered if Paula had really seen Flora. Maybe Paula was in on it with her sister and Myron and they were trying to point the finger in Flora's direction. And what about Ed? I didn't dare mention my suspicions about him to Mom and Millie; they'd known him for years and would defend him as they had Flora. I didn't want the killer to be Ed either. Myron and Carla were much better suspects in my book.

The crunch of tires on gravel pulled my gaze to the window. Mom and Millie were here and I couldn't wait to tell them what I'd discovered.

I heard the kitchen door open and then Millie's voice. "Josie, is something burning?"

Chapter Twenty

I rushed in to the kitchen to see Millie rescuing the loaf pan from the oven. She put it on the counter and waved the smoke away, then sniffed.

"Oh, it's the apple-pecan bread." Then she sniffed deeper. "I think it needs more cinnamon. How long did you put it in for?"

"Ninety minutes just like your recipe said." I gestured toward the timer on the microwave still ticking down. "It still has ten minutes."

Millie looked at me as if she felt sorry for me. "Josie, that time was for a full loaf pan. You have to reduce it for the smaller pans."

Darn. Who knew that you cooked things for less time when they are in a smaller pan? I probably should have. Lucky thing I'd decided to start small with my experiment and I still had some of the batter left. Besides, we had more pressing matters to discuss.

"Never mind about that." I glanced back out into the hallway to make sure none of the Biddefords had followed me in. "I think I've discovered something."

"Do tell," Millie said.

"Remember how Myron lied about being here the night Bob was killed?"

"Yep." Millie tasted the batter I'd mixed, then puckered her lips and rummaged in the spice drawer.

"Do you know where he went to college?"

Mom huffed. "Who could forget? He went to Yale. His father always made a big deal out of that, making the rest of us feel like our kids were inferior."

"Why do you ask?" Millie sprinkled some cinnamon into the batter, grabbed a spoon and mixed it in.

"Well, Carla went to Yale too. She even has a mug that she makes me wash out so she can drink out of it. That's how I put two and two together when I washed the mug this morning." I hadn't done that all on my own, though. Nero had practically pushed that mug off the counter. Had he been trying to point me in the right direction? Or had he just been trying to smash the mug on the floor because he also thought it was ridiculous that Carla brought her own mug?

"So you think they knew each other?" Mom asked.

I nodded and opened the oven door for Millie to slide in the two tiny loaf pans she'd filled with batter. I made a mental note as she set the timer to thirty-five minutes.

Millie shut the oven door, a twinkle in her eye. "We found out something about Myron last night too. His ancestor was Jedediah Biddeford's butler."

"I found that too! In the history book that you wanted me to bring for the table at the town celebration." The cats had been interested in that book as well. Except it had seemed like they *didn't* want me to read it. Maybe I was reading too much into their actions?

Millie's face fell in disappointment. "You already knew?"

I nodded, pushing down the pang of guilt at Millie and Mom's looks of disappointment. Investigating was a source of pride for them and they clearly didn't like the idea that I'd also discovered their key clue.

Millie broke into a genuine smile and turned to my mother. "Josie is turning into a good detective. We should include her in all our cases."

Cases? It sounded as if they were contemplating becoming private investigators or something.

I held my hands up in front of me, palms out. "I think I have plenty to do just running the guesthouse."

Mom looked me over as if I were an unworthy job applicant. "I don't know. I suppose she might come in handy to drive us around while we interrogate suspects and look for clues."

"Can we stick to the problem at hand?" The last thing I wanted to do with my days was drive my mother and Millie around. Hopefully this would be the last murder Oyster Cove would see for a long time and there would be no need to investigate anything in the future anyway.

Millie pressed her lips together. "Fine. Myron might have gone to school with Carla and his ancestor was Jed's butler. Why would they kill Bob?"

"Well, I was thinking that a butler would know all the secrets of his master and maybe Myron's ancestor knew where the treasure was buried. Maybe that information got passed down in the family and Myron came to dig it up."

Millie and Mom looked at each other and shook their heads.

"Maybe Josie isn't a good fit for our investigative exploits after all," Mom said.

"Yeah, your theory is full of holes," Millie added.

I crossed my arms over my chest. "How so?"

"Well, for one, if Myron's family already knew where the treasure was, why wouldn't someone have dug it up before?" Millie asked.

"And for two," my mother added, "why would he need to combine forces with Carla?"

They had a point, but I wasn't letting go of my theory that easily. "Maybe the family didn't know where the treasure was all this time, but the discovery of Jed's skeleton and the curse rumor resurfacing prompted Myron to look through some family documents and he found something that made him think he knew where the treasure was."

"He did seem awfully interested in that skeleton," Millie said.

"And he did lie about being here, which means he was up to something," Mom added. "But what's the connection to Carla?"

"Maybe they were rekindling an old affair," I suggested.

Millie leaned in toward us and lowered her voice. "Can't say as I'd blame her, her husband doesn't seem like much fun."

"And Bob did threaten to tell on her about something. But why wouldn't she just divorce Henry then? Bob outing an affair doesn't seem worth killing over,"

Mom said, then added, "I have another theory, maybe whatever Myron found wasn't a precise location and he needed some family information from Carla to narrow it down so they partnered up."

"And Bob found out and was going to steal the treasure so they did him in," Millie added. "That makes sense."

"Do you think there really is treasure then?" Mom asked.

Millie shrugged. "Good question. I doubt it because if Myron and Carla dug it up, they'd have taken off together, wouldn't they?"

"Treasure or not, it's something to look into," Mom said. "Flora is still a suspect and we need to help Seth close this one fast before those rumors about this place being haunted spread too far and hurt bookings."

Millie tapped her finger on her lips. "Indeed. But how can we approach Seth with this? He's already suspicious of any clues I give him because he thinks we are biased as to Flora's innocence."

"I know the dates that Carla and Myron were at Yale, which proves they could have known each other," I said.

"Yes, but that's not concrete evidence. We need something more."

Mom snapped her fingers. "The shoes! Paula saw fancy Italian leather shoes. Earl was wearing Nikes but he's not the only one who likes to dress fancy."

Millie put her hands on her hips. "Those could have been Myron's shoes she saw."

"So all we have to do is get Paula to identify the

shoes, preferably while Myron is wearing them and in front of Seth Chamberlain so that he'll have his physical evidence," I said.

"Easier said than done," Millie said, peeking into the oven to check on the loaf cake. "We need to get Paula to run into Myron somehow when Carla isn't around."

"I know how we can do it," Mom said. "The beer tent is open today and they're having free samples. All we have to do is mention that to Paula and drop the hint that we are on our way to the beer tent, then offer to give her a ride."

Millie nodded. "And once we're down there, we will just take a little stroll past Myron's bank table. I know he's there today trying to trap tourists into investing in something at the bank."

"But how do we get Seth in on this?" I asked.

Millie whipped out her phone. "Easy. I'll call him and bribe him to come and meet us there. I just happen to have some of his favorite cookies in the car."

Chapter Twenty-One

"I think the beer tent is over there." Paula twisted around, pointing in a direction behind us and almost stumbling as she pulled her heel out from where it had sunk into the grass. I grabbed her elbow to steady her.

"I know. We're just going this way to get our free tickets," Millie said as we propelled her toward Myron's tent.

Millie glanced at me behind Paula's back and grimaced for telling the lie. A little white lie was necessary sometimes in an investigation. Still, Paula wouldn't miss out on her free beer—she'd be well rewarded *after* she identified Myron's shoes to Seth. Hopefully Myron would be wearing the same ones, or at least something similar that Paula would recognize and spark Seth's suspicions.

"I hope Jed's ghost doesn't show up here." Paula scanned the crowd. "Though I guess he won't be after me. I didn't take any treasure. I wonder if Bob did? And if he did maybe Jed took it back because no one's found it yet and Bob certainly didn't take it with him. So if Jed took it, there won't be any more killings because he'll have his treasure and the curse will be broken."

Paula's train of thought was pretty logical even if it was a bit rambling, but my mother glanced over at her as if she were crazy. "I doubt it was Jed who killed Bob."

"Well, that's the rumor I heard," Paula huffed. "Who else could it be? Certainly not your maid that I saw running from the scene. She's too old, now that I think of it." Paula frowned as if considering her own words. "Or maybe it *was* your maid. Some of those old people are pretty strong."

Flora had been acting strangely. I had no idea if she actually was strong enough to have clobbered Bob, but I saw her move the antique carved-mahogany couch out from the wall to get behind it with the vacuum, so she was pretty strong. And what was this business with the vacation?

But if Flora had stolen the treasure why would she still be hanging around the guesthouse? Unless she hadn't actually *found* the treasure and Bob's murder was for nothing. What was I thinking? Flora wouldn't kill someone, no matter how valuable a treasure was involved.

Up ahead at Myron's table, I saw a familiar figure lurking about. Annabel Drescher stood in front of one of the plastic displays that held interest-rate information. She snatched a pamphlet out and looked around furtively. I caught her eye and waved, but she pretended not to notice me. Maybe she didn't want to be seen associating with someone whose maid was accused of murder?

"Looks like Arlene has some competition." Paula's gaze was pinned on Annabel as she walked away. "Fancy duds and even shoes like Earl's."

Wait, what? I swivel around to check out Annabel's shoes. Paula was right, they were Italian leather similar to Earl's. Suddenly I was second-guessing my Carla–Myron theory. Maybe Flora wasn't lying about the vacation. But why would Annabel make that up... unless she was trying to cover something up or distract us.

"Oh look, you can get a home-equity line of credit for three percent, maybe you should tap into that for the renovations?" Millie's comment redirected my attention from Annabel to Myron's table.

Paula inspected the pamphlets closer, her eyes clouding over in confusion. "Where are the tickets for the beer tent?"

"Beer tent?" Myron's eyes darted from Paula to me. "Are you interested in a loan?"

I glanced around for Seth. Millie had said he'd be meeting us here and we had to stall until he showed up so we could get Paula to identify the shoes in front of him. Mom jabbed me in the ribs and jerked her head toward the big display touting the low-interest-rate loans. Guess that would be a good way to stall.

"As a matter fact I am," I said. It wasn't totally a lie, either. Extra money would help me complete the renovations sooner. Too bad I didn't actually have much money to make the payments until business picked up. It was a catch twenty-two. I needed the loan to accommodate more guests, but I needed more guests to pay the monthly rate on the loan. "You know, I have that whole west wing over at the Oyster Cove Guesthouse and the sooner I can get it renovated the sooner I can get more guests in. Do you have anything special, preferably with a delayed payment schedule?"

Approval radiated from Millie at my quick reaction, but before Myron could launch into his spiel, Seth showed up.

"Hello, ladies." Seth nodded at each of us, but his gaze lingered on Millie.

"I made your favorites, Seth." Millie held up the bag of cookies and opened it, tipping the bag forward so we could all see inside. She tipped the bag further forward, letting one cookie slide out onto the grass as if by accident. "Oh, dear me. I've dropped one."

She dropped to her knees and made a show of rooting around in the grass under the table for the cookie. "What lovely shoes, Myron. You're always such a sharp dresser."

Myron tugged at his tie uncomfortably, a look of confusion crossing his face. "Um ... thanks."

Millie tugged on Paula's arm. It didn't take much to get her to stumble and Millie pulled her down so she could see Myron's shoes. "Aren't those lovely, Paula?"

"Sure, they're very nice but I don't see any beer-tent tickets."

"We'll get to the beer tent. Don't you worry about that. But do these shoes look a little familiar to you?" Millie asked.

Myron shot up from his seat. "What is the meaning of this? Why are you so interested in my shoes?"

Seth was watching carefully. He might seem like a dunderhead, but he actually could be rather sharp sometimes. He'd caught on that Millie had an ulterior motive here and was smart enough to keep quiet and see where this would lead. Perhaps all of Mom and

Millie's meddling in his investigations really had given him respect for their skills.

"Familiar?" Paula stumbled to her feet and glanced around behind us. "If there's no tickets I'm just going to—"

"Take another look, Paula," Millie said. "I think these might be the shoes that woke you up the night Bob was murdered."

Paula's eyes widened. She bent down again to look at the shoes. She scrunched up her face, closed her eyes and then opened them one at a time. "Well, they are fine Italian leather like the ones I saw. Very similar. Let me see the backs. I mostly saw the backs as the person was running away."

"I certainly will not." Myron looked at Seth. "Do I have to?"

Seth shrugged. "What's the harm? Unless you have something to hide."

Myron marched out from behind the table and spun around.

Paula nodded. "Yep, very similar to the shoes I saw."

"Similar? Or are they *exactly* the shoes?" Seth asked.

"Well, I can't say for sure. I mean I was just waking up and my memory is fuzzy. There are a lot of fancy shoes like these, in fact I saw a woman wearing similar shoes earlier." Paula glanced in the direction that Annabel had gone.

"She's not a reliable witness. I heard that she's drunk all the time!" Myron said.

"I'm not drunk *all* the time." Paula crossed her arms over her chest.

"I demand to know what this is about." Myron looked at Seth.

"Paula saw someone running from where the murder happened and they wore expensive shoes," Seth said. "Apparently Millie here is playing amateur detective and thinks Paula might recognize the shoes as yours."

"Running from where the murder happened? But that was centuries ago, why I couldn't..." Myron's face relaxed a little. "Oh! You mean the recent murder, not the skeleton they found in the wall."

"Of course. That's what we're investigating. Can't really investigate a murder from three centuries ago."

Myron blew out a breath. "Well, that's ridiculous. Why would I kill one of the Biddefords?"

"You have a family connection to the Biddefords," Mom said.

Myron made a face. "Yeah, about three hundred years back. What would that have to do with anything recent?"

"There was treasure rumored to be buried there," Millie said. "Maybe one of your ancestors knew where it was and when you went to dig it up Bob had gotten there first."

Myron laughed. "You believe that treasure rumor? What would I want with some old moldy treasure chest that probably doesn't have anything of modern value in it? I have plenty of money. I own a bank. And besides, I wouldn't waste my time. That treasure doesn't even exist according to *my* family lore."

Did Myron have some family intel about the treasure or was he just saying that as a cover?

"Why did you lie about being there then?" I asked.

Myron turned sheepish. He glanced around to make sure none of the other people in the tent were listening. "I had a good reason—that stupid treasure hunt actually messed it up. I was there, but not because of the treasure." He glanced at Seth. "I have proof. Normally I'd make you get a search warrant, but I'm not guilty and I want you to stop accusing me and find the real killer, so I'd be happy to show it to you."

Millie looked skeptical. "You would? That's a little fishy. If you really have a reason, seems like you'd be more irate about being accused."

"Oh, I am. But I don't want to ruin the bank's reputation, which would happen if a crowd witnessed you accusing me, or worse, hauling me off in cuffs."

"Okay, let me see this proof," Seth said.

"Me too," Millie added.

"Not *you*." Myron glared at Millie. "You're just a civilian and it's none of your business. Just the sheriff."

Paula crossed her arms over her chest and pouted at Millie. "You said we were going to get free beer at the beer tent."

"I'll take you," Mom said, and headed off with Paula.

Seth leveled a look at me and Millie. "Well, you heard the man. We don't need civilians seeing someone's private business."

"Come on, Josie, let's go look over there at the Frobusher's local honey display." She shot a coquettish glance at Seth and batted her eyelashes before pulling me aside and whispering in my ear. "I'll get it out of him later, but for now let's just let Myron show it to him."

We wandered away, both keeping an eye on Seth and Myron. Myron showed him something on his cell phone and Seth nodded approvingly. Darn! Whatever Myron was showing him must've satisfied Seth.

Seth started walking away and Millie did an about-face. "*Yoo-hoo*, Sethy!" She summoned him over in her most provocative manner. "Now, I know it's probably a big secret and all, but I don't think it would hurt if you could tell us what Myron showed you."

She walked her fingers up his arm playfully. Seth smiled but took her hand away gently.

"I can't tell you, but I can tell you one thing: he does have proof of why he was there and that proof has a timestamp of when the coroner has told us Bob was killed. The pond is a fifteen-minute walk from the gazebo in the daytime, probably longer in the dark, and we all know Myron is no woodsman. It would take him an hour to get through the thick overgrowth. I don't think he could be the killer."

"So, it must have been one of the Biddefords," Millie said.

Seth's face turned solemn. "I don't think so."

"Why?" Millie asked.

"We processed all of the shovels we took from the carriage house. There were six shovels in the shed, one for each member of the Biddeford family, except Bob whose shovel was found next to him at the murder scene. And not one of them has any DNA from Bob on the metal end—the blade. The coroner has determined Bob was killed with the metal part of the shovel, but the only shovel that matched his DNA was the one Bob used, and that only had epithelia on the handle. Nothing on the blade, which substantiates Doris Biddeford's claim that Bob took off on his own but the rest of them stayed together."

"He wasn't killed with one of the shovels in the carriage house?" I asked. Something about Doris's claim didn't sit right. Hadn't she asked the others at breakfast, before Bob's body was found, if anyone found the treasure? If they all stayed together she would have known if anything was found. Had she lied to the police?

Seth shook his head. "Nope. He was killed with another shovel, so the murder weapon must be out there somewhere."

"Half the town had shovels, the store was sold out," I said. Everyone except Myron, who had said he couldn't get one because Flora had gotten the last one. Which made me wonder…where was Flora's shovel? Had she taken it home or was it on the premises somewhere?

"That's right," Seth agreed. "But I am afraid half the town was *not* seen running from the scene by an eyewitness—only one person was. And that person is now my main suspect."

"Seth Chamberlain, you can't be serious!" Millie said. "What motive would she have?"

"That remains to be seen." A look of regret passed over Seth's face. "Unfortunately, unless new evidence comes to light, I'm going to be bringing Flora in for questioning and you better hope there isn't another shovel out there with her fingerprints on one end and Bob's DNA on the other."

Chapter Twenty-Two

"It simply can't be Flora," Millie insisted later on when we were back in the kitchen of the Oyster Cove Guesthouse. She was vigorously beating together batter for a new batch of apple-pecan bread with extra cinnamon. "She's been with the guesthouse since I was a little girl. My parents hired her. She's a great-grandma, for crying out loud!"

It was just the two of us in the kitchen since my mom had texted that she and Paula had found a ride home from the beer tent and were staying for a few more. Apparently Paula was good company over a mug of beer.

Millie had actually stayed behind too, to try to wrangle more information out of Seth, and I'd driven home by myself. He'd dropped her off at the guesthouse a little bit later.

"I don't know." I hesitated. "A lot of the clues do point to her."

I didn't *want* it to be Flora. Even though she was the world's worst maid, she was starting to grow on me. She had a certain grandmotherly way about her, sort of like Sophia from *The Golden Girls,* but grumpier.

Even so, I had to admit some things about Flora's story didn't add up. Then again, I'd just added a few suspects to my mental suspect list. "I have my suspicions about a few other people too."

Millie turned to look at me. "Really? Who?"

"Annabel Drescher, for one. Paula said her shoes were like Earl's and she is doing a lot of renovations on her travel agency, so might need treasure-money. Plus, it seemed like she was avoiding us and Flora said she never went in to book a vacation. Maybe Annabel has something to hide."

Millie considered this, then shook her head. "Kind of far-fetched that she would kill Bob but I'll keep her in mind. Who is the other person?"

"Ed O'Hara."

"Ed? You must be joking. Why he's the nicest man you'd want to meet. He wouldn't hurt a fly. Why do you suspect him?"

That was true, but wasn't it always the nice ones that turned out to be the killer? "I think he was sneaking around in the conservatory."

"The conservatory? What's that got to do with any of this? That part of the house wasn't even built back in Jed's day and besides, don't you have work for him in there?"

"Yes, but he wasn't supposed to be doing that yet."

Millie scowled at me. "I think you are grasping at straws. Do you have some reason to think Ed being in the conservatory has something to do with Bob's death? Or the treasure?"

She had a point. All I had was a nail that could have gotten in there in a dozen ways. I guess I *was* getting carried away.

Millie must have taken my silence for agreement because she went back to considering the Biddefords as prime suspects. "Just because those shovels didn't have any of Bob's blood on them doesn't mean one of the Biddefords isn't the killer." Millie beat the batter more vigorously.

"True. I mean, if they were clever, they could have clonked him over the head and switched shovels. Besides, I think Doris lied about them all being together." I much preferred Doris as a suspect over Ed anyway. "But then where is the shovel that killed Bob? And where is Flora's?"

"I don't know, seems like Seth would have confiscated it from her if he thinks she's a suspect." Millie paused her beating and turned to me. "Do you think Doris lied because she killed her son?"

"I'm not sure. She was pretty upset about the business failing and Bob was threatening everyone. If he made good on any of those threats, it wouldn't be good for business," I said. "Maybe she thought that the treasure curse and ghost would make a good cover. Someone has been pushing that ghost rumor pretty hard around town."

"Would Doris really think that Seth would believe that a ghost killed someone?"

Millie and I exchanged a glance. Seth wasn't the sharpest pencil but I didn't think he believed in murdering ghosts. But maybe Doris thought he did.

"We have to figure out what is going on with Flora." The missing shovel bothered me. Seth had said the Biddefords' shovels had been tested and none of them had been used to kill Bob. If Doris was the killer, then how had she pulled that off? On the other hand, Flora had been making herself scarce around the guesthouse lately. Was that so she could avoid Seth because she knew that he was going to ask for her shovel?

"But *why* would she kill Bob? I doubt there is even any treasure and she never mentioned needing money," Millie said, almost to herself. "Maybe I should've given her a raise before I sold the guesthouse."

Was I not paying Flora enough? But she barely did anything. I made a mental note to give her a raise anyway once profits increased. If she wasn't rotting away in a jail cell.

"Myron could have used a shovel from home. I mean just because the store was sold out doesn't mean a thing. I'm sure there are some shovels hanging around that big estate he lives on. Maybe his proof that he showed Seth was fake?" I said.

"Oh, that." Millie fluffed her hair, her cheeks turning crimson. "I got that out of Seth behind the Chamber of Commerce tent."

Best not to ask what she'd had to do behind the tent to get it out of him. "So what was it?"

Millie grabbed a loaf pan and started pouring the batter in. "Apparently one of your guests is taking out a loan to buy out more than fifty percent of the stock in the cheese-sculpting business."

"Seriously?" This was big news. Why hadn't she mentioned that when she first came in?

"Yeah, I thought it was important too, but it's not

because it clears Myron as well as one of the Biddefords. And it also proves that Doris is lying."

"Wait, one of them was going to steal the company out from under the rest of the family? Was it Bob? Is that why he was killed because someone found out and wanted to stop him from taking control?"

It wasn't totally ridiculous. After all, the company was failing and the siblings were at odds. It did seem prudent for one of them to buy the others out, take control and dictate a course of action that might bring the company back to its former glory. At least, I hoped so for Doris's sake. "But why would they get a loan from a bank all the way out here? Their business is in New Jersey."

"Turns out you were partially right about Myron and Carla. They did know each other from Yale. They weren't having an affair, though; she prevailed upon him to get this loan because she didn't want to go with anyone local to them because she wanted secrecy." Millie glanced around to make sure no Biddefords were lurking within hearing distance. "You can imagine what a ruckus that would cause if the family found out someone was attempting a hostile takeover."

"Yeah. I can't imagine that Bob would have liked it much. I wonder if that's what Bob was threatening her about?"

"It could've been. But I don't think she's the one who killed Bob because Seth said it's one of those online documents that you sign electronically and it's time-stamped. Apparently, that's why they didn't go to the bank and did the dirty deed here in the gazebo." Millie shoved the pan into the oven. "Carla already knew her family would be digging outside and that they wouldn't be anywhere near the gazebo since that wasn't built in Jed's day. She figured it would be the perfect place to meet him without her family asking a lot of questions about where she was going. They'd all be focused on where they thought the treasure was and no one would be paying much attention to her. The timestamp is shortly before the time of death for Bob, so that gives both Myron and Carla an alibi. Seth said there was no way they could have gotten from the gazebo to the pond that quickly."

"Unless they signed it while they were killing Bob. How does he even know they were actually at the gazebo?" I asked.

"GPS coordinates," Millie said. "Besides, what motive would they have? Once the papers were signed Carla could buy the stock and it would all be out in the open anyway, so Bob telling on her was no threat. And Myron got to sell a loan so he wouldn't care about Bob."

"Good point, but the cats were specifically showing me…" I looked around the room. "Hey, where are the cats?" They usually ran in at the first sight of Millie.

"Probably napping somewhere or outside with their friends."

I frowned remembering the cats I'd seen at the crime scene. Were Nero and Marlowe in some kind of cat gang?

"What were you saying about the cats anyway, dear?" Millie continued.

"Oh, nothing. I just sort of thought that maybe they were pointing me toward Myron and Carla."

"Oh, they might have been. Nero and Marlowe are very perceptive. They know things. And of course they see things that humans can't see. But even if they were pointing you toward Myron and Carla, it could've been to tell you that you were on the wrong track," Millie said wisely.

"Great. Well, this doesn't help us clear Flora."

"I know. That is a problem, but I'm sure she must have an explanation for all these things that appear to point to her. Things are not always as they seem, you know."

The kitchen door opened and Mike strode in with my mom giggling behind him. He shot me an apologetic glance. "I found your mom dancing down at the beer tent. Seemed like it was a good idea to take her home."

Mom slouched into a kitchen chair and hiccupped out a sentence. "Yeah. That Oyster Rock Brew sure has a kick to it."

"New local beer," Mike said by way of explanation.

Mom cradled her head in her arms on the table and Millie said, "I'll make a pot of coffee."

Mike smiled at my mom then turned his pearly whites on me. "This brings back memories, Sunshine. Like the time I found you drunk in a beer tent back in high school. I think that was the first time you went drinking. You acted a lot like your mom is now. Except when you—"

"Never mind that," I cut him off. That day had not been one of my finest moments. I didn't want to remember how Mike had saved my ass by dragging me out of that beer tent where I was holding court with a bunch of college guys.

Truth be told, I was grateful he'd barged in and pulled me away, but my memories of the actual events were a bit fuzzy. I had the ridiculous feeling that he'd kissed me that day, but I wasn't a hundred percent sure. Even so, my cheeks burned and my heartbeat sped up when my gaze met his.

Was Mike's memory of that day the same as mine? I saw something flicker in his eyes, then his gaze turned suspicious. "So, what were you guys up to down there?"

Millie's expression was all fake innocence and sweetness. "Whatever do you mean? We were simply making sure the Oyster Cove Guesthouse table was set up properly."

"Uh huh." Mike looked like he didn't believe a word. "And that's why you needed to bring Paula? She's upstairs passed out by the way. I drove her home with Rose." He leaned against the counter nonchalantly, folding his arms over his chest. "And why were you over at Myron's table with Paula and Sheriff Chamberlain?"

How did he know that? Had he been spying on us?

"They just happened to be there too." Millie averted her gaze and pretended like she was checking on the loaf pan.

"Interesting. I just hope you aren't up to something you shouldn't be. The sheriff is perfectly capable of conducting an investigation."

Millie sighed. "Of course he is. You don't think we're trying to figure out who killed Bob Biddeford on our own, do you? I mean if we were, we'd ask for your help."

Mike didn't look like he was buying Millie's song and dance in the least.

"He should join forces with *ushh* and *weed* find the killers *fashter*," Mom slurred. Her head was resting on her arms atop the table but she'd turned it sideways to look at us.

"Aha!" Mike said. "I knew it."

"Knew what? We're just baking a loaf cake." I pointed at the oven. "She's drunk. Doesn't know what she's saying."

Mom frowned at me but was smart enough to hold her tongue.

"I'm not the enemy here and I'm not trying to ruin your fun. I just don't want you to get hurt. Any of you." His eyes drifted from Mom to Millie and then settled on me. "You're all very precious to me."

"Don't worry, dear. We'll be careful," Millie said. "I don't need to remind you that Rose, Josie and I are mature adults and don't need you telling us what to do."

Mike threw up his hands in exasperation. "Fine. I know I can't tell you what to do. But I just hope you won't get into any serious trouble."

He pinned me with his gaze, but to his credit didn't elaborate as to how we should back off on the investigation—or worse—how we should leave it to a professional like him.

"Yes, dear, and thank you for bringing Rose back." Millie pushed him out the door. "I know you're very busy downtown with your new job and all, so we'll let you get back to it."

Mike paused at the door and turned to me. "I'll be back later to double-check the foundation and walls under the conservatory."

He would? That was news to me. "Now? Ed won't be starting in there for a while."

He looked at me funny. "I think you might be focusing too much on investigating and not enough on what is going on in your own guesthouse. Some structural work was done to the walls already and I need to make sure it didn't affect anything because of the weird way they constructed that room."

Again, news to me. "What weird way?" Wait! Ed had already done something in there?

"When they added the conservatory, they used the wall of an existing barn that was adjacent to the house. That old barn had been original to the property. Did you notice that the foundation underneath is giant slabs of granite?"

I nodded.

"You can't find those anymore. Anyway, since that existing wall and foundation is so old, I want to check the structural integrity before too much more work gets done." Mike glanced at his watch then grimaced. "Gotta run. Have to inspect an addition over at the old Dunkirk place."

Mike shot a smile in my direction and went out the door as I digested this new tidbit of information. Not only had Ed lied about being in the conservatory, but the foundation and one of the walls dated back to Jed's time. My thoughts drifted back to the conversation between the Biddefords right after we'd discovered the skeleton. They'd been talking about looking for a map and wondering if one could have been in the wall with Jed. Doris had said she'd looked in there pretty good, but she hadn't seen a map and since they'd all arrived at the same time none of them could have taken it without the others seeing. The thing was, there was one person who had been there before any of us and that person could have taken the map. Ed.

I looked up at my mother and Millie, a feeling of dread blooming in my stomach. "I think we better go talk to Ed."

*

Nero, Marlowe and the other cats crouched under an azalea bush, inspecting the shovel that protruded halfway out of the ground. There was no doubt why it had been buried. The coppery scent of blood and murderous intent hung maliciously in the air. A faint breeze rustled the leaves, the only sound breaking the silence as the cats watched Harry carefully brush away some of the dirt.

Nero was proud of Harry and the others. They'd sniffed around the grounds and uncovered this valuable clue, then ran to gather him and Marlowe from the guesthouse. Now it had been carefully uncovered just enough so that they could lead the humans over to discover it on their own.

"Yep, that's the murder weapon all right." Harry sat back on his haunches and licked his paw, clearly satisfied with his own detective work.

"I can smell Bob's blood on the end." Juliette's face wrinkled in distaste. "But I don't smell the woman who made the confession."

"So she's not the killer." Nero paced around the shovel,

sniffing at it from all angles. Some of it was still buried, but his superior senses could sniff out the lingering scents even below the earth. Unfortunately, those scents did not provide clues as to who had wielded the weapon.

Marlowe glanced back in the direction of the guesthouse. "How are we going to get Josie out here to find a shovel?"

"Good question," Nero said.

Boots looked at him with his usual air of superiority and Nero resisted the urge to hiss at the other cat. He knew Boots was mostly jealous of Nero's superior skills of deduction, not to mention that Nero had white tuxedo markings on his chest while Boots only had white on his paws. The tuxedo gave Nero a debonair air and Boots had always been a little jealous.

"I thought Josie was starting to come around?" Stubbs said.

Nero sighed. "She is a work in progress. She is starting to become aware of our communication attempts. Why, just this morning I pushed her toward a clue about Carla Biddeford's mug and I know for a fact she understood the mug was a clue."

"She's not up to speed yet, though," Marlowe added. "Last night she misconstrued our communications and even though she knew the mug was a clue, we aren't sure she realized what we meant by it."

"True," Nero mused. "Perhaps it would be best if we try to bring Millie."

"Millie is certainly a possibility." Boots tugged at his whiskers. "But does Millie have enough clues to figure out who the killer is?"

Juliette swiped her paw toward the shovel. "The murder weapon seems like a big enough clue. I'm sure the police can do forensics on it and figure out who the killer is."

Boots sniffed and turned up his nose. "Their lab tests are far inferior to our feline senses."

"Is that so?" Harry asked. "Then you tell me. *Who* is the killer?"

"Well…err…" Boots glanced around the area. "There isn't enough evidence to say. Having said that, are we sure Millie will even want to present the murder weapon to Sheriff Chamberlain?"

"What do you mean, will she want to? Of course she will, because it may prove who the killer is," Marlowe said.

"Precisely my point," Boots said. "What if the killer is someone Millie does not want revealed? Someone she is very close to and has a vested interest in protecting."

Nero's heart dropped at the thought. Normally he would never even think that Millie would shield a killer from the law. But Millie was loyal to those she loved and Nero knew that Sheriff Chamberlain had Flora on his suspect list. But it couldn't be Flora, Nero was sure of it. He was a good judge of character and beneath Flora's gruff exterior was a kind heart. Never mind that she'd lied about a few things and never mind that her shoes had smelled like burned loaf cakes. She simply couldn't be the killer. But that begged the question… who was?

"Well, one thing we know is it ain't no ghost," Stubbs said.

Nero would have laughed, if laughing wasn't beneath him. "Of course not. Although half the town thinks it is. If there was a ghost, we would be seeing it."

It was common knowledge that cats could see spirits from other planes, though humans seemed to find the idea hard to grasp. What did they think the cats were doing when they stared at the wall or into the corner, apparently at nothing? Since Nero hadn't seen a ghost at the guesthouse, he was confident that Jed's spirit had not returned.

"But that means the killer is much more dangerous. A human. A human who thinks he or she is getting away with murder," Harry said.

Nero's expression was grim as he looked down at the shovel. "We need to bring this to the attention of the humans before it's too late. If my guess is correct, the killer is planning to dispose of it once the heat dies down."

A rustling in the bushes startled them and they turned, ears like radar dishes figuring out what made the sound.

"Uh oh," Poe said. "Looks like we may be too late. Unless I'm totally off my game, that's the killer and they've come back to find a better hiding spot for the murder weapon."

Chapter Twenty-Three

Ed should have been working in the west wing, but he wasn't. We searched the house, finally bumping into him as he came in the back door that led to the overgrown gardens. He seemed surprised to see us and possibly a little bit guilty as he wiped off wet hands on his jeans.

"So, where have you been?" I asked.

A flicker of surprise at my accusing tone passed over his kindly face and I was speared with guilt. Was I jumping to conclusions?

"I was out by the water spigot washing off my paintbrushes. I started doing the trim work in the game room. Would you like to see?"

"Not right now." I glanced back at Millie. I probably should have prepared a line of questioning or something, but I hadn't and suddenly didn't know what to say. Thankfully Millie took over.

"Ed, we were just talking to Mike and he mentioned something odd about the conservatory," Millie said.

Ed straightened, his eyes narrowing. Aha! I hadn't been jumping to conclusions.

"What do you mean?" he asked.

"Well, Josie here says that you haven't done any work in there yet."

Ed couldn't meet my eyes. Or Millie's. "That's right."

"But Mike said he was inspecting some work you'd done for structural integrity."

Ed bit his lip but remained silent.

I took that as guilt. "Ed, what were you doing in there? Does it have anything to do with the treasure or the murder?"

Ed's eyes widened. "What? No! Why would you ask that?"

I glanced at Millie. Mom was leaning against the wall, her eyes half closed. She was no help. Ed sounded genuinely surprised at my question. "Well, it's obvious you are up to something. You lied to me. Why else would you do that?"

Ed sighed, his shoulders slumping. "Okay, fine. I admit I lied. But it was what you'd call one of them little white lies."

A little white lie? About murder and treasure stealing?

Millie patted Ed's arm. "Of course it was. Now, why don't you tell us all about it so Josie can get rid of this silly notion that you had something to do with the murder." She shot me a see-I-told-you-Ed-wouldn't-do-anything-wrong look.

"Fine, but it will ruin the surprise. Better that I show you." Ed gestured toward the hallway and we all started walking.

I had to admit, I wasn't as convinced of Ed's innocence as Millie was. He was leading us toward the conservatory and my mind kept telling me to run. If Ed was the killer and knew that we'd figured it out, wouldn't he want to kill us next? Then again, he was an old man and we were three women. Well, two and a half if you consider my mother wasn't operating at full speed. I figured we could take him and didn't I owe him the chance to prove me wrong?

Millie didn't seem the least bit worried and followed him right into the conservatory. I hung back in the doorway imagining how the conservatory, which had most of its windows boarded up and was in an isolated part of the house, was a great place to murder someone without being seen. Remaining in the doorway seemed like a good plan because then I could run if he tried something. There was no way I was going to let him get me inside the room and shut the door.

But then Ed did something surprising. He headed over to one of the windows and ripped off the plywood.

Mom, Millie and I gasped.

Underneath the plywood, the windows had been replaced and Ed had installed gorgeous hand-carved molding that was a replica of the original, now rotten, wood.

"Oh! It looks delightful!" Millie squealed.

Ed blushed and revealed the next window, and the next.

This is what he'd lied about?

Mom and I wandered into the room for a closer look. The wood was oak, stained and polished to honeyed perfection. The carvings were vines and flowers. The artistry was stunning. I turned to Ed. "Did you carve these?"

His cheeks reddened even further and he nodded.

"Got nothing much else to do now that the missus is gone."

"But why did you lie about it?" I asked.

"It was supposed to be a surprise. I was going to wait until I had all the windows done and show you all at once."

I pushed words out around the lump of guilt that had formed in my throat: "Thank you. This is really above and beyond anything I was expecting."

I couldn't believe that Ed had done all this and I hadn't been aware. Maybe I had been too focused on my lack of cooking skills. In my defense, the conservatory was in a secluded section of the guesthouse and he had done most of the work in his shop at home. I wouldn't have heard the hammering. And since the gardens outside were incredibly overgrown, I never went back there so never noticed the windows had been replaced.

I ran my hand over the woodwork. "I'm sorry I suspected you."

Ed looked down at his feet. "That's okay. But why did you suspect me?"

I explained about the wall being original and how I'd thought maybe he had taken a map out of the wall we'd found Jed's skeleton in and it had led to this area.

He shook his head. "Nope. No map. If I was a thief I'd have taken that ring, not some map. But now I wonder if that's why she was acting so sneaky and secretive."

"She?" Mom, Millie and I said in unison. Even Mom had perked up for that.

"Flora. I saw her coming out of one of the guest

rooms and she was shoving something in her pocket and looking around to see if anyone was watching. She didn't see me because I'd just come down from the attic stairs in the back. I can't be a hundred-percent sure, but I could have sworn she was muttering something about it being the strangest map she ever saw."

Chapter Twenty-Four

We found Flora in the front parlor dusting, if you consider sitting on the sofa and running the feather duster over the coffee table while watching the TV dusting.

She must've known something was up, though, because she eyed us suspiciously as we approached.

"What? I'm working on my break." Flora seemed indignant. "You should be lucky I'm just not sitting watching TV. I get a fifteen-minute break every two hours. Federal law."

I glanced at Millie. Was that really true? Didn't matter right now, we had more important fish to fry.

"It's not about that, Flora," I said.

Flora's eyes got a little bigger behind the round glasses. She stopped dusting and fiddled with the feathers. "Well, what is it? I cleaned that room like you asked me to."

Millie sat down next to her and took her hand. Flora suddenly became very interested in the floor, the window, the table...anything so she didn't have to look at us. "Well, what is it? Spit it out if you have something to say." The tone in her voice didn't match the gruff words. It was clear that Flora was hiding something. I hoped it wasn't the fact that she'd killed Bob.

"Now, Flora, we've known each other for a long

time," Millie said soothingly. "And you know you can tell me the truth."

"The truth? I always tell the truth." But the way Flora couldn't meet Millie's eyes seemed to indicate that this was not the case. My stomach swooped. Had we been wrong about her?

"Maybe sometimes you tell a little white lie or omit things," Millie persisted. "Like when you said you weren't out digging earlier but then admitted later on to Josie that you were in fact out there."

Flora scowled. "I never said I wasn't out *digging*. I said I wouldn't have the strength to bash someone over the head with a shovel. You people need to learn how to listen. Why don't you ask your boyfriend if you want the truth."

Millie blushed.

Mom snorted.

Flora smirked.

"But that's not the only thing you were evasive about, is it?" I asked.

Flora jerked her hand away from Millie and crossed her arms over her chest. "I'm not a liar. I might have a bad memory, though. What, exactly, are you talking about?"

"You lied about cleaning Arlene and Earl's room. I saw you go in there and Ed saw you acting sneaky when you came out." I didn't mention the part about him thinking she was hiding something in her pocket and mumbling about a map. Stealing from a guest's room was a harsh accusation and Ed hadn't seemed completely certain. If Flora had taken something, I wanted to give her the chance to admit to it on her own. "And you lied about not having a shovel."

"*And* you lied about taking a vacation," Mom said. "Annabel at the travel agency said that you were looking to go to the Caribbean."

Flora looked at Mom like she was crazy. "The Caribbean? Where in tarnation did she ever get that idea?" She turned her gaze on me. "I don't appreciate you calling me a liar, either. And that Ed is a tattletale."

"Well, then explain all this," I said. "Why are you being so evasive about being near the pond? What were you doing at the travel agency? Why were you sneaking around Earl and Arlene's room? And *where* is your shovel?"

Flora straightened on the couch, looking rather indignant. Her eyes drifted from me to Millie and then to my mother. Her mouth worked up and down. "I… I…"

Finally, she sighed and collapsed back into the couch. "Okay, maybe I told a little lie about one of these things."

"So you *were* running from the pond the night Bob was killed?" I said.

"Sort of. Well, I was near there, but I didn't kill Bob." Flora looked contrite and picked at the feathers in the duster. "Let me explain."

"Okay. That's a relief. I knew you couldn't kill anyone anyway." Millie patted her hand.

"When I heard there was treasure, I figured why not try to dig it up too, so I went out there with the rest of them. I was following the family members around thinking they might have a lead on the location. That's how I ended up on the path from the pond."

Millie and Mom scooted to the edges of their seats. "So you were there before Bob was killed? Did you see him with someone or hear them arguing?"

"No, I didn't see him at all. It was kind of dark and…well, I don't see as good as I used to. For all I know, Bob was already dead when I went past." Flora blanched. "Oh dear, I hope he wasn't flopping around and I could've helped him. Truth was it was a little scary out there and I was rushing back toward the house."

"You didn't see anyone rushing away. No one in front of you?" Mom asked.

"No." Flora still couldn't meet our eyes. There was something she wasn't telling us.

"But you must've seen something. Sheriff Chamberlain thinks you're the killer so anything you know would be really helpful in your defense," Millie said.

"I didn't see anything, I swear. If you ask me it's one of those family members. They were all arguing with Bob."

"Yeah, we know that. But, Flora, think hard. You must have seen something," I said.

"Nope." She gazed out the window.

"Okay, what about your shovel? Where did you put that? Maybe if we can give the shovel to Seth he can do some testing on it to rule you out," Millie suggested.

Flora gave her a funny look. "*Give* it to Seth? He already has it. I'm surprised he still suspects me. Seems like he could have figured out my shovel isn't the one that killed Bob. Then again, that boy always was a little slow on the uptake."

"You already gave him the shovel? When?" I didn't see how she could have possibly done that in between the time we saw Seth at the town celebration and now, especially since she'd been here cleaning the whole time and Seth hadn't stopped by. But at the celebration Seth still suspected her, so he must not have had it yet.

"Give it to him? No. I saw him take it. I put it in the carriage house with the rest of the shovels. That's where you said you wanted people to put them."

My brows knit together. "You did? But Sheriff Chamberlain only found six shovels, one for each of the Biddefords, besides Bob. His shovel was at the murder scene."

Mom jumped out of her chair. "Seth just assumed all those belonged to the Biddefords, but if one of the shovels was Flora's then that means one of the Biddefords' shovels is missing. My guess is that is the murder weapon!"

"Which means that Flora is cleared because Seth himself said none of those shovels were the murder weapon," Millie said.

"And that also means that one of the Biddefords really is the killer," I said. Or could it still be Annabel? But if it was her, why would one of the Biddefords' shovels be missing?

"But which one?" Mom asked.

"I hate to say it, but Doris said she'd do anything to get the company back on track and she also lied about them all being together that night," I said.

"Bob argued with Carla but she seems to have an alibi," Mom said.

"Paula also argued with Bob," Millie pointed out. "And Paula has been trying to frame quite a few people. Flora and then Myron with the shoes. Maybe she's the real killer."

"I heard someone else argue with Bob," Flora said.

We swiveled our heads in her direction. "Who?"

"Earl," she said.

"What did they argue about?" I asked.

"It's not like I was trying to eavesdrop. You were out shopping and I was cleaning the hallway when Bob burst into Earl's room. They had a little bit of a tiff. I couldn't hear too good but it sounded like something about a secret book and rubble. I figured the rubble had to do with digging, that's why I . . ."

Flora's voice trailed off and she got more fidgety with the feather duster and glanced around the room.

"You what?" I prompted.

"Okay, okay! I'll admit it. I was lying about one thing. I didn't clean Earl and Arlene's room that day, but I *was* in there."

"What were you doing?" Millie asked.

Flora glanced around to make sure no one else was about, then continued, "When I heard the argument about the secret book I assumed it was something about a treasure map. You know, maybe an old family book or something? I figured it wouldn't do any harm to go in there and while I was cleaning maybe I could find this book." Flora glanced out the window. "But when I went in it was pretty obvious where the treasure map was."

"Wait, there really is a map?" I could practically see my mom thinking about rushing home to get a shovel.

News of the map plus Millie's coffee had sobered her up.

"Well, there *was*. Problem is Earl had burned most of it in the fireplace in his room. I could make out nothing but a few lines of longitude and latitude." Flora's expression turned sheepish. "I lied because I didn't want you to think I stole from the room."

"Really? If Earl knew where the treasure was, then did he dig it up?" Millie said.

"If Bob and Earl argued over it maybe only Bob knew where it was," Mom said. "Maybe that's why it was burned."

"Wait a minute. I want to see this map. Do you still have it?" I asked.

Flora blanched. "It wasn't really stealing, honest. I mean it was in the fireplace so technically it was trash and I was just taking out the trash."

"Of course. I'm not mad you took it, but I would like to look at it," I said.

"It's right here in my pocket." Flora produced a wrinkled, charred piece of paper. "It won't do you any good, though. The map wasn't for anything on this property. I think Jedediah might've buried his treasure at sea."

"Why do you say that?" I asked. Millie and Mom had come to stand behind me so they could look over my shoulder.

"I went down to the travel agency lady to find out where these longitude and latitude would be. But this stupid map isn't for this property—she said it was for somewhere in the Caribbean Ocean!"

Millie glanced at me. "Annabel wasn't lying. Flora really was there, she just assumed she was looking to take a vacation because of the longitude and latitude."

"But why would Jed bury the treasure in the middle of the ocean?" Mom's eyes narrowed. "What if Annabel really did lie? What if she lied to Flora about the coordinates?"

"What do you mean?" Flora asked.

Mom leaned forward in her seat. "What if Annabel recognized the numbers for what they were—a map to the treasure. And what if she didn't want anyone else to know the location. She might have given Flora false information about what the longitude and latitude really meant so that she could dig up the treasure herself!"

Millie pressed her lips together. "Hmmm…she did have those fancy shoes and she is expanding her business which means she got an influx of money."

I stared down at the paper. It was a column of numbers that reminded me of the unbalanced accounting ledger I had for the guesthouse. "Are you sure these are longitude and latitude? Because they don't look like it to me."

"They don't? Well, I just assumed they were. I mean, why talk about a secret book and then burn the paper?" Flora asked.

Something else tickled the back of my brain. I was on to something, but had one more question. "Flora, did you clean Millie's grandmother's doily in the parlor the morning that Sheriff Chamberlain interviewed all of us?"

"No, I actually didn't clean that. I know I should have corrected you when you thanked me for cleaning it before, but I figured what the heck, if you thought I did extra work who am I to set you straight? Besides, after Sheriff Chamberlain interrogated me I had to go to my friend's house to bake cookies for the great-grandmothers of twins' table at the town celebration."

If Flora didn't clean the doily, then why had it been clean when there were clumps of dirt on the table? Of course! It was all coming together. "I think I know who the killer is and if we can just find that missing shovel, we can prove—"

Meroowl!

At the panicked sound of a cat's cry, we whipped our heads around to see Nero standing in the doorway. His fur was puffed and his tail stood straight up as his large golden eyes beseeched us.

Millie frowned. "I never see Nero alone. Nero, where is Marlowe?"

Nero gave an ungodly cry, spun around and raced out of the room.

Millie, Mom and I were on our feet in a second, following the cat. It was clear by the way Nero was acting that something was dreadfully wrong.

Chapter Twenty-Five

Millie was the first through the kitchen door, with my mother and me close behind. Who knew Millie could move so fast? I had to hand it to Mom too, she was managing to keep up despite the afternoon in the beer tent with Paula.

"Marlowe must be in trouble!" Millie yelled as we watched Nero's tail disappear down the path that led to the old gardening shed. My mind conjured up all the bad things that could happen to a cat out there. Had she fallen through old rotted boards? Cut herself on a rusty tool? Gotten stuck in some old animal trap? Fallen into an abandoned well? The thought of poor Marlowe hurt was crushing.

As we headed deeper into the overgrown area, I glanced behind me. Flora was making a good effort to keep up but had barely made it down the back steps. She waved me on and I turned forward, running to catch up to Mom and Millie.

Branches whipped in our faces as we jumped over gnarled roots sticking up out of the ground and side-stepped fallen branches. We heard a voice ahead.

"Hey, get off, you mangy fur ball!"
Meow!
Millie and Mom had sprinted ahead. They skidded

to a stop and I just barely missed bowling them over. My eyes immediately scanned for Marlowe. She was caterwauling loudly and her fur was standing on end, but she seemed fine. It was kind of hard to tell for sure, though, because she was latched onto a pant leg and the owner of said leg was trying vigorously to kick her off.

The cats I had seen at the murder scene were all there, too. Their backs were humped and tails fluffed out like bottle brushes. Some were hissing as they stood between the person and the bloody shovel sticking partway out of the ground.

The murder weapon!

"Marlowe!" Millie was aghast. "Leave him alone. I'm so sorry, the cats don't usually act this way."

Apparently Millie hadn't put two and two together yet. The cats weren't attacking for no reason. They'd captured the killer—Earl Biddeford.

I felt momentary satisfaction that my suspicions had been correct. I was about to name Earl as the killer when Nero had interrupted with his caterwauling. I hadn't been a hundred-percent positive then. I was now.

"I don't know why she's acting this way..." Millie wrung her hands, probably picturing a lawsuit.

"She's acting that way because he is the killer." I stepped between Earl and the shovel, standing next to the cats, my arms crossed over my chest to signify that there was no way Earl was going to get to that shovel.

"He is?" Mom turned to me.

"Yes, he is. Isn't that right, Earl?"

Earl forgot about Marlowe, who was still digging in

to his leg, and turned malicious eyes on me. "You three busybodies should have left well enough alone! You should have let everyone think it was Jedediah's ghost."

"Why would we do that? Bob deserved to have his killer caught." I inched to the left, hoping Mom and Millie got the hint to surround him. It looked like the cats did too because they started to fan out. The black cat with the white paws seemed a bit reluctant but the orange-striped one with the missing tail looked like he was itching to dig his claws into Earl's other leg.

"He didn't deserve anything! He was a slacker. Always weaseling out of work. His sculptures were sub-par. He couldn't even carve a decent swan." Earl tried to step toward me but was weighed down by the cat on his leg.

"But that's not why you killed him, is it?" I inched my way further to the left.

"No. His lack of skills wasn't the reason. Bob was always a tattletale. I'm surprised someone else didn't do him in before me." Earl twisted to try to get rid of Marlowe. My blood froze. Tucked in the back of Earl's pants was a gun. I had to tread very carefully. Hopefully, I could keep him distracted with talking.

"I never did like a tattletale," Mom said.

"No one does," Earl said. "I did everyone a favor."

"But you mostly did yourself a favor, didn't you? Because Bob had something on you that would pit your entire family against you and probably send you to jail."

"You mean the secret book with the treasure map?" Mom asked.

"No. There was a secret book, but it wasn't about

treasure. Earl was embezzling from the company." I looked at Earl. "Weren't you?"

Millie snapped her fingers. "Of course! I should have known. I thought it was odd that Earl and Arlene always dressed to the nines given that the company was having trouble."

I pointed toward Earl's feet. He was wearing fancy Italian loafers. "It really was your shoes that Paula saw running away from the pond, wasn't it?"

"Stupid Paula. Leave it to her to be passed out right in my getaway path," Earl said. "I chose that pond area because I knew no one was over there. No witnesses."

I shifted to the left, still trying to surround him. Millie was over on the right but unfortunately my mother appeared oblivious to the plan. She was shuffling from foot to foot and looking a bit uncomfortable.

"That wasn't the only flaw in your plan," I said. "Oh, you almost had us fooled. I mean, who would suspect you had a reason to kill Bob, especially after you burned the real accounting ledger in your fireplace."

I smiled at the look of surprise on Earl's face. "Yeah, the maid found the evidence and we have it safe and sound at the guesthouse for the police."

Earl looked skeptical. "What? There must only be a few small scraps left. Nothing that would prove anything except that I burned some paper with numbers. By the way, you should look into getting a new maid. That one's work leaves a bit to be desired."

I ignored his comment about Flora. It's not like it was anything I didn't already know. "You made another key mistake, too."

"What? Picking a guesthouse with you three nosy people at it?"

"Well, that too, but when you brought the Nikes down to prove that it wasn't your shoes that Paula saw, you made a big error. I worked out that you put that dirt on them not from outside, but from the plants in the conservatory. But you messed up."

"How?"

"You only put dirt on the tops! If you'd really been wearing them, the dirt would have been clumped into the treads and have fallen out on the table, but dirt only came off the sides. The actual spot where the soles had been was clean." And that explained why the doily had not been dirty. Turned out Flora's reluctance to clean most things provided a key clue to catching the killer.

"And now we have the murder weapon," Millie said, pointing at the shovel. "I would say your cheese-sculpting days are over. You might as well just give up. Play nice and you might get a reduced sentence. I'll just call the sheriff and tell him—"

"Not so fast!" Earl pulled the gun out of his pocket and waved it around. "I'm not going to jail."

"Now, Earl, be careful with that thing. You don't want to go to jail for multiple murders." Millie glanced over at me as if to ask what our plan was now. I didn't have one other than not getting shot.

"Why not? If I'm going for one anyway, how much time can it add?" Earl laughed. "But I'm not going for even one. Too bad you're all so nosy. I had the perfect setup here, especially once that skeleton was discovered.

I mean, who gets a chance to frame a ghost? And if that didn't work, I could always let your maid take the rap."

"Well, that's not going to work. Not once they get this shovel to the CSI lab and find your fingerprints and Bob's blood on it," Millie said.

"Not gonna happen. If only these stupid cats didn't dig it up. Actually, maybe it's a good thing they did. I'll need something to dig the hole to bury your bodies in."

Mom raised her hand. "Can I go to the little girls' room?"

"No. You won't need to worry about that soon."

My heart stopped as he stepped toward my mother, pointing the gun at her head.

Meroooo!

A blur of black-and-white shot toward Earl's gun arm. Nero!

"Ouch!" Earl shook his arm, but he didn't drop the gun.

My mind whirled with indecision. Should I lunge toward the gun? Go for his knees and knock him down? He was still holding the darn gun!

There was a rustle in the bushes behind him. A thick branch appeared, crashing down on Earl's head. He crumpled to the ground.

Behind him stood Flora. She looked down at Earl's still body.

"Guess I lied about another thing," she said.

"What?" Millie asked.

Flora nudged Earl's arm with her toe. "Looks like this old bird really does have the strength to clonk someone over the head."

Millie hugged her. "You saved the day."

"Ahh, it was nothing," Flora said.

"Thanks, Flora. I gotta make a pit stop." Mom ducked behind a shrub.

Nero and Marlowe trotted over to me and rubbed against my ankles. "Thanks, guys." I picked them up one by one and buried my face in their fur. When I put them back down, they trotted over to Millie. It didn't escape me that they'd come to me first.

"I better call Seth before Earl wakes up. He is alive, isn't he?" asked Millie.

"Yep." I'd already done a visual check to make sure he was still breathing.

"That's a relief. Didn't want Flora to be accused of murder again."

Mom reappeared from behind the bush and I noticed that while Nero and Marlowe were sticking close by, the other cats had disappeared. I guess they didn't want to hang around and take credit for discovering the murder weapon. Just like Millie had always said, there was more to the cats than met the eye—and not just Nero and Marlowe.

Millie dialed. Then she made a face, her eyes squinting and her nose wrinkling. She turned in the direction of the guesthouse and sniffed the air. "Say, do I smell something burning?"

Chapter Twenty-Six

"Josie, this is the most delicious apple-pecan bread I've ever tasted!" Annabel Drescher stood in front of my table chewing noisily on one of the tiny loaves of bread.

I'd burned another test loaf when we'd been busy capturing Earl. But I'd finally nailed the recipe for the bread, and fifty-four miniature loaves were stacked in a pyramid in the middle of the Oyster Cove Guesthouse display table at Oyster Cove's 250th town celebration. The tent and streets were crowded and the mood was festive.

From inside the tents, which were nestled on the lush green grass of the town common, shaded by stately oaks and maples, one could see the quaint shops that lined Main Street in one direction, and the sparkling blue ocean in the other.

The Oyster Cove Chamber of Commerce had outdone themselves decorating for the festivities. A large banner with an image of the town two centuries ago hung across the street. Various food vendors and carnival games had been set up on the other side of the town common across from the shops, which all had sparkling clean windows and vibrant awnings. Baskets overflowing with colorful flowers hung from the fancy wrought-iron lampposts that lined the streets. The air was spiced with the scent of popcorn, the sounds of laughter and the cry of an occasional gull.

"Thank you. Josie is a fine baker." Millie sat proudly in the chair beside me. It was generous of her to give me credit since she was the reason they were so delicious, but I wasn't about to argue.

Annabel took another bite and leaned across the table, glancing over at Stella out of the corner of her eye.

"Much better than Stella Dumont's custard…that tasted sour," she whispered.

"I knew it would," Millie muttered under her breath.

"Lucky for Myron he gave me that loan for my travel agency instead of giving one to Stella," Annabel said.

"Yeah, lucky." I felt bad for suspecting her. It turned out she really hadn't lied about Flora. Flora really had gone there with numbers, except they weren't longitude and latitude, they were accounting numbers which had correlated with a longitude and latitude in the Caribbean Sea. Annabel had no idea what the numbers really were, though, and had just made an assumption that Flora wanted a vacation. She hadn't dug up treasure to renovate her travel agency, she'd gotten a loan.

I simply smiled and nodded, then glanced over at the Smugglers Bay Inn table. People were milling about in front of it, but no one was eating the custard. I wondered if she'd gotten any bookings.

There were plenty of tourists in town and some of them might want to make a reservation to come back. Hopefully the curdling custard would drive more tourists toward my place, though I wasn't particularly worried. I'd gotten quite a number of reservations in the past few days.

"You haven't cut the cheese yet?" Mom gestured toward the towering sculpture that dominated the right side of the table. It was a likeness of the Oyster Cove Guesthouse as it was 250 years ago, carved out of cheddar.

Doris had secretly whipped it up after I'd given her permission to bury Jed's skeleton in the old family cemetery on the property. Unfortunately, the burial never happened. With the logistics of getting into the overgrown part of the estate, heavy equipment to dig up the yard and state regulations, the Biddefords decided it was too costly and had opted for cremation. Doris said she'd rather use the money for a good rehab place for Paula.

Doris had handled Earl's arrest well. I had to admire her; finding out one of your sons murdered another one couldn't be easy. It turned out she had had her suspicions that one of her children had killed Bob from the beginning; that's why she'd lied to Seth when she'd told him they'd all stuck together that night. She was hoping to provide an alibi for her kids.

But she was making the best of it, and at least something good had come from it. It seemed to have brought Doris, Paula and Carla closer together. Doris was taking back the reins of the cheese-sculpture business. She was determined to run it the right way and restore it to its former glory.

I suspected her gift of the sculpture wasn't totally unselfish—she'd conveniently presented it to me under the tent and suggested I put it on my table with some of her business cards, just in case someone wanted to order a cheese sculpture of their own. I was happy to drum up business for her after everything she'd been through.

"Seems a shame to cut it, don't you think?" I said. Doris had nicely provided crackers, but I couldn't bring myself to cut into the sculpture. Besides, it was attracting people, and that was good for business—both mine and the Biddefords'.

"Yeah, but I'm hungry. Maybe I'll just pinch off one of the shrubberies here," Mom said, bending down and presumably looking for an inconspicuous spot to pinch some cheese.

A splash followed by a round of laughter caught our attention and we looked over to the mayor's head surfacing from the dunk tank. I'd heard dunking the mayor had been a very popular attraction and since the money people paid for a chance went to the Chamber of Commerce festivals fund, he was being a good sport about it.

"Looking for Jed's ghost in there?" Myron nodded at the sculpture. Apparently, he'd wandered over when my attention was on the dunk tank. As much as I would have liked to tell him to get lost, I couldn't. He had approached me with the terms of a loan that I didn't have to start paying on for twelve months. That meant I could step up renovations and get the guesthouse fully functional a lot sooner. Unfortunately, it also meant I'd have to be nice to Myron.

"Hardly." Mom pinched off a corner and plopped it onto a cracker. "You don't believe in ghosts, do you?"

Myron shook his head. "Nope. And I don't believe there's treasure either. At least not from what my grandfather told me."

"We never thought there was any treasure," Millie said. "I think I would have known if there was something valuable right under my very nose."

"Naturally. My relatives would have known if Jed had buried any treasure. I just hope this whole business with finding Jed's skeleton and the rumor of his ghost doesn't dissuade people from staying at the guesthouse." Myron winked at me and I tried not to make a face. "I have a vested interest in it now."

"Don't worry, Myron. People haven't been put off by the skeleton. Quite the opposite, in fact. Several of the people who made reservations specifically asked if it was the place where Jedediah Biddeford's skeleton was found so, apparently, that helps business not hurts it."

"That's good." Myron picked up an apple-pecan loaf. "Say, did they ever send the skeleton to that forensic anthropologist your daughter mentioned?"

"No. The Biddefords are having him cremated."

"Statute of limitation ran out on that case, anyway." Seth Chamberlain had come up, along with Mike Sullivan. The two of them paused to let a small gang of children grasping pink and blue clouds of cotton candy on sticks run in front of them.

"So you won't be running around, trying to investigate that murder, then?" Myron said.

Myron had taken an interest in the guesthouse because of his ancestral ties to it. He said he wanted to embrace his humble beginnings and that was why he'd give me the loan, though Mom and Millie thought it was because he was sweet on me. I guess that's why he was so interested in the investigation in the first place. I felt a little sad that Jed's murder would never be solved, but if the police weren't going to look into it, who would?

"Nope. We'll be investigating the murder of Bob Biddeford, although that one is pretty cut and dried," Seth said. "We found the evidence we needed on that shovel and since the three of you heard him confess, it's a slam dunk."

"And you won't need to disrupt the guests in the guesthouse, right?" Millie asked.

Seth looked at her with twinkling eyes. "Nope. Josie is free to run it unencumbered by a police investigation."

"And since she'll be having so much construction done with the new loan, I'll be spending a lot of time over there inspecting it," Mike said.

I wasn't sure I liked the non-businesslike look he gave me when he said that. Or the way my mother's eyebrows waggled up and down. Or the smug look on Millie's face. Before I could say anything, Ed O'Hara came up and broke a piece of porch railing off the cheese sculpture.

"And I'll have work for a long time." Ed looked at me fondly...maybe a little too fondly. "Congratulations on catching the killer by the way."

"It wasn't just me. I had a lot of help." I gestured to my mother and Millie. Even though I really *was* the one who had figured out who killed Bob, I could be modest when I wanted to be.

"Yeah, and you were on the wrong track, Seth," Millie said.

"Right. See, we can investigate and not get ourselves in trouble." My mother shot a pointed look at Mike.

"Yeah. See?" I added, also giving Mike a look just to drive the point home.

Mike held his hands up in a gesture of surrender. "Okay, I admit you guys did manage to capture him. But he had a gun, you could have been shot."

"But we weren't. Flora was the real hero anyway. She clonked him over the head and saved the day!" Millie turned to Seth. "And to think, you suspected her."

"Nah...I knew she wasn't the real killer and that the truth would come out in the end," Seth said.

Millie scrunched up her face. "You expect us to believe that? You said you were going to bring her in for questioning. Why, I bet you were about to arrest her when we called telling you we'd caught the real killer. Without us you might have arrested the wrong person for the murder."

"Yeah," my mother said. "You needed us to put it all together for you. We don't mind doing it this time, but next time I hope you'll be able to do some of the work yourself. I mean, you can't expect us to solve all the murders that happen in this town, can he, Josie?"

"I'm sure Sheriff Chamberlain can do just fine without our help."

Seth was taking it all in his stride. A movement behind him caught my eye. Nero and Marlowe were skulking around the edges of the tent, heading toward the town docks.

It had been kind of fun figuring out who had killed Bob, but I hoped we wouldn't have another murder in town anytime soon. We hadn't totally figured it all out on our own, either. I was starting to realize that we'd had a little non-human help. As if sensing my thoughts, Nero turned and looked right at me.

Yep, I was sure we'd gotten more than a little help from the cats. But I couldn't very well tell anyone that, now could I?

*

"Too bad the humans will never realize the key role we played in helping them find the killer," Nero said as they trotted past the tents on their way to the bait wharf.

"I don't know, I think Josie has an idea. I mean, she must have figured out that I was hanging on to Earl's leg for a reason," Marlowe said. "But I suppose she can't very well go around telling people that her cats helped her solve a murder."

They rounded the side of the harbormaster's station and proceeded straight to the bait wharf. All the other cats were lounging around by the lobster traps. No fish scraps this time, Nero noted with disappointment. Maybe they could persuade Josie and Millie to give them some morsels from the cheese sculpture later.

"Louie Two Paws tells me the case against Earl is pretty much tied up," Harry said. His police informant— a double-pawed Siamese—always had interesting and invaluable information from the station.

"Yep. I think we did well," Nero said as he hopped onto a lobster trap.

"And finally Josie is starting to realize that it pays to listen to us," Marlowe noted, flopping down in the sun.

"And the confession I overheard?" Juliette asked.

"That was Carla. She wanted to cleanse her soul in regards to her sneaky plan to take over the company," Nero said.

"But it's all worked out because now Doris, Carla and Paula will run the company. Since Earl was embezzling most of the money, the company's financial situation isn't as dire as they thought," Marlowe said.

"They can get the company back on track and it's all thanks to us," Boots preened.

"Right," Stubbs said. "By catching Earl, we exposed his embezzling and saved the company."

"And we cleared Flora," Nero said. "You know, I knew her shoes smelled like something burnt. At first I suspected it had something to do with all the breads Josie was burning. Turns out she was rooting around in Earl's fireplace for what she thought was a treasure map."

"Who knew she was actually listening to the argument we overheard between Bob and Earl that day in the hallway? I thought she was dusting," Marlowe said.

"Sometimes things are not always as you think," Nero said wisely. The truth was that he also had thought Flora was just dusting but he wanted to make it seem like he knew more.

"And that also explains why the dirt on the table in the foyer smelled so familiar," Marlowe said.

Juliette frowned. "What do you mean?"

"Earl claimed he wasn't wearing the Ferragamo shoes that Paula saw the night of the murder. He produced a pair of mud-caked Nikes to prove it."

"But it turned out the dirt on the Nikes was from

the pot of the ficus tree in the conservatory," Nero
added. "When Earl was accused, he snuck down to the
conservatory and dirtied his sneakers. The dirt was still
on the table in the foyer where he'd presented them to
Sheriff Chamberlain. I just wish we'd sniffed that one
out sooner. Could have cracked the case earlier."

"Well, the important thing is that we did crack the
case," Poe said.

"Yep. And Josie even has a full house of guests next
week and more money for renovations." Nero watched
a lobster boat motoring out of the narrow mouth of the
cove on its way to the open ocean. "There is something
odd about the new guests."

Juliette sat up, her interest piqued. "Odd? How?"

"They seemed unusually interested in assuring
themselves that the Oyster Cove Guesthouse was the
guesthouse where Jedediah's skeleton was found," Nero
said.

"Why would they want to do that?" Stubbs asked.

"One reason," Harry said. "They're interested in
ghosts."

"But there is no ghost," Marlowe pointed out.

Nero shrugged. "I guess they will discover that in
due time. For now, Josie has a full roster of bookings
and that's what counts."

Poe plopped down on the warm ground. "And now
we can rest."

"I will miss having guests with cheese," Marlowe
said. "But hopefully the next guests will be able to keep
from killing each other."

Boots looked down his long whiskers at Marlowe

with an expression that indicated she had a lot to learn. "I wouldn't be too sure about that. Josie doesn't have a very good track record in the murder department. And if recent history is any indication, we may need to keep a close eye on the next batch of guests."

A Letter from Leighann

Hi! I hope you enjoyed *A Whisker in the Dark*. If you did enjoy it and want to keep up-to-date with all my latest releases, just sign up at the following link. Your email address will never be shared and you can unsubscribe at any time.

http://www.leighanndobbs.com/

In the book, Josie burns a lot of baked goods. I have to admit that I have experience with that myself! My mother, on the other hand, was a great baker and I have so many fond childhood memories of sitting in her kitchen while she baked. My mom is gone now, but the recipes in this series are from her old cookbooks and recipe cards that I inherited. Even the descriptions of the food-stained cards written in faded blue ink are the actual descriptions of her cards.

Another food aspect of the book is the cheese sculpting—yes, that is a thing! Did you know that the largest ever cheese sculpture weighed over 1,500 pounds and was in the form of a cheeseburger sculpted out of Wisconsin cheddar? I wonder how long it would take Nero and Marlowe to snack on that?

All best,
Lee

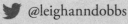 @leighanndobbs

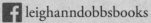 leighanndobbsbooks

www.leighanndobbs.com

Recipes

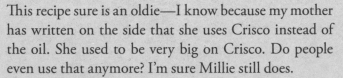

Pumpkin Bread

This recipe sure is an oldie—I know because my mother has written on the side that she uses Crisco instead of the oil. She used to be very big on Crisco. Do people even use that anymore? I'm sure Millie still does.

Makes 3 loaf pans.

Ingredients:

- 4 eggs
- 1 cup oil (or if you're like my mom, you'll want to use 1 cup shortening)
- ⅔ cup water
- 2 cups canned pumpkin (a 14 or 16 oz can)
- 3 ⅓ cups all-purpose flour
- 2 ½ cups sugar
- ½ teaspoon salt
- 2 teaspoons baking soda
- 1 teaspoon nutmeg
- 1 teaspoon cinnamon
- A pinch of ground cloves
- 1 cup chopped walnuts (optional)

Directions:

1. Heat oven to 350 degrees F or 177 degrees C.
2. Combine eggs, oil (or shortening), water, and pumpkin in a large bowl and mix well.

3. Sift flour and add sugar, salt, baking soda, nutmeg, cinnamon, and cloves.
4. Combine wet and dry ingredients and mix well.
5. Turn into 3 greased loaf pans (regular size) and bake for 45 minutes.

Broccoli Quiche

Millie likes to prepare this the night before and slide it into the oven to warm up the next morning for breakfast.

The recipe claims this serves 3. It's a 9-inch pie plate, though, so those are some big servings!

Ingredients:
- 3 eggs
- 3 oz cheddar cheese, grated
- 10 oz package frozen broccoli (cooked)
- ⅛ teaspoon pepper
- 1 ½ cups cooked rice
- ¾ teaspoon salt
- 6 tablespoons skim milk

Optional: add ¾ cup drained cooked mushrooms. Heck, while you are at it, you could add some ham or bacon too. Maybe even some spinach or chopped peppers.

Directions:
1. Heat oven to 375 degrees F or 190 degrees C.
2. Beat 1 egg. Add the rice, ½ the grated cheese and salt. Mix well, then press firmly in an even layer on the bottom of a 9-inch pie plate.
3. Beat remaining eggs slightly. Stir in broccoli, milk, pepper, and whatever else you are adding, plus the rest of the cheese.
4. Bake for 30 minutes.

◤ *Peanut-Butter-Banana Bread* ◥

This recipe is actually a low-calorie one I found in my mother's stash. It says each serving is only 28 calories, but I'm skeptical about that. Then again, it doesn't say the serving size so maybe it's only a crumb.

Ingredients:

- ♥ 6 tablespoons peanut butter
- ♥ 2 teaspoons reduced-calorie margarine *(Margarine? Yech! This recipe is from the seventies when margarine was all the rage. I'd use butter.)*
- ♥ ⅛ cup skim milk
- ♥ ⅛ cup water
- ♥ 1 banana, mashed
- ♥ ½ cup nonfat powdered milk
- ♥ 10 teaspoons low-calorie sweetener *(I'd use Truvia but they didn't have that back when Mom wrote this recipe)*
- ♥ 1 teaspoon brown sugar
- ♥ ½ teaspoon baking soda
- ♥ 2 teaspoons baking powder
- ♥ 9 tablespoons all-purpose flour

Directions:

1. Heat oven to 350 degrees F or 177 degrees C.
2. Mix peanut butter and margarine together, then stir in mashed banana. Add skim milk and water.

3. Combine dry ingredients, then mix into peanut-butter-banana mixture.
4. Pour into a greased loaf pan.
5. Bake for 30 minutes.

Apple-Pecan Bread

This thing takes forever to cook but I'd start checking early if I were you... you wouldn't want it to burn!

Ingredients:
- 3 eggs
- 1 teaspoon vanilla
- 1 cup oil
- 2 cups sugar
- 3 cups all-purpose flour
- 1 teaspoon baking soda
- 1 teaspoon salt
- 1 teaspoon cinnamon
- 3 cups apples, diced
- 1 cup pecans, chopped

Directions:
1. Heat oven to 300 degrees F or 150 degrees C.
2. Beat eggs, oil and vanilla.
3. Combine sugar, flour, baking soda, salt, and cinnamon. Add egg mixture and stir well. Batter will be very thick. Fold in apples and pecans.
4. Divide batter into 2 greased 9x5x3-inch loaf pans.
5. Bake for 90 minutes.

USA Today bestselling author Leighann Dobbs discovered her passion for writing after a twenty-year career as a software engineer. She lives in New Hampshire with her husband, Bruce, their trusty Chihuahua mix, Mojo, and their beautiful rescue cat, Kitty. When she's not reading, gardening, making jewelry, or selling antiques, she likes to write cozy mystery and historical romance books.

Learn more about Leighann Dobbs at:
leighanndobbs.com
Facebook.com/leighanndobbsbooks
Twitter @Leighanndobbs

ISBN 978-1-5387-3621-0

73621

UPC
S

"Is that one of those adorable cats you have here?"
Adorable? I supposed they were sort of cute when they
weren't pushing things off the counter or ripping the
toilet paper off the roll…or finding dead bodies.

Discovering the three-hundred-year-old skeleton of shipping tycoon Jedediah Biddeford in a wall is a big old hassle for Josie Waters, owner of the Oyster Cove Guesthouse. Especially when Biddeford's descendants turn up, certain that a family legend about treasure buried nearby must be true.

Josie is too busy dreaming up the perfect cake for Oyster Cove's two-hundred-fiftieth anniversary celebration to worry about the Biddeford family—plus half the town—digging up her yard…until one of her guests is murdered in the garden.

With worries that her guesthouse will get a reputation for being the kind of place you only leave in a body bag, Josie must put her detective skills to work to find the killer. Lucky for her, Nero and Marlowe and their gang of cat sleuths are also on the case.

GrandCentralPublishing.com
Cover design: Debbie Clement.
Cover images: Shutterstock
Cover © 2021 Hachette Book Group, Inc.
Printed in the U.S.A.

$8.99 US / $12.99 CAN.
ISBN 978-1-5387-3621-0

EAN

9 781538 736210   50899